TROPICAL WOUNDED WOLF

ZOE CHANT

SHIFTING SANDS RESORT

This book is part of a complete series, with recurring characters, but it does stand alone, with a satisfying happy-ever-after and no cliffhangers. Escape to Shifting Sands Resort and buckle up for a ten-book binge-read that will take you on a wild ride with a thrilling conclusion!

See also: the Shifting Sands Resort Omnibus, 4 volumes that include all the books, short stories, novellas, and three exclusive stories, all in the author's preferred reading order, available in ebook, paperback, audiobook, and hardcover!

CHAPTER 1

"*I* cannot vacation at a *nude* resort," Mary North said in horror. "I even have to change into my swimsuit in a toilet stall at the health club."

Her co-worker Alice, a bear shifter, rolled her eyes. "It's not nude, it's *clothing-optional*. There's a big difference and if you're shy, you spend the whole time in animal form."

"Oh, I don't know," Mary sighed. "The pictures are lovely, but I'm not sure I like the idea of a shifters-only resort. It's in a foreign country and they have poisonous snakes there, probably. Plus, two women traveling alone? We might get robbed, or kidnapped!" She shuddered dramatically, and sniffed the coffee pot cautiously. Like the deer she could shift into, Mary was wary of everything. She suspected that the pot had been sitting out for hours on the burner.

"I'm sure they don't have poisonous snakes at a fancy all-inclusive place like Shifting Sands Resort," Alice scoffed. "And it's not like Costa Rica is some third world nation. Did you see the photo of the pool?"

"I did," Mary admitted wistfully. She loved swimming

and the brochure made the pool look amazing: huge and crystal-blue in the sparkling sunshine, with pseudo-Greek columns, waterfalls, and palm trees around it.

"And the snorkeling!"

"I couldn't swim in the *ocean*," Mary said swiftly, deciding to dump the coffee out and wait for a new pot. She had just enough time before the next block of classes to brew one.

Alice snagged a cup before she could pour all of the coffee out, but Alice lived dangerously like that.

"Have you ever been in the ocean?" Alice asked, taking a sip of the molten sludge.

"They have sharks in the ocean! And stinging jellyfish and *eels* and things. Besides, this resort sounds expensive." Mary measured the coffee grounds carefully, shaking each scoop perfectly level.

"It's not so bad, once you realize that you don't have to pay for any food. It even includes massages and kayak rentals and guided hikes..."

"A tippy little kayak out on the ocean? You have to be kidding me!"

"... And I know you aren't spending your whole salary, living like you do. You haven't taken a vacation in years."

Mary smiled down at her second hand outfit. Alice wasn't wrong about her spending habits, and she did have a nice little nest egg put aside specifically for a vacation someday.

Still...

"I'm not sure. It's so far away!"

"That's a great deal of its charm," Alice said dryly. "And I'll be with you, so it's not like you'd be going alone! I speak Spanish like a native, and I can protect you from eels and poisonous snakes and strange men."

"But..."

Alice shook her coffee cup threateningly at Mary. "If you don't come with me, I will undoubtedly do something reckless and regrettable, and you will have to live with the guilt of not being with me to keep me from being foolish forever."

"I can't even keep you from drinking terrible coffee," Mary said plaintively, pouring her own fresh cup as the ancient coffee pot beeped its tired announcement of completion.

Alice grinned, probably sensing her victory. "But at least you won't have the guilt of not trying hanging over your head." She drained the last of her bitter cup defiantly, just as the class warning bell rang.

Mary blew at her superior java as she gathered her teaching plan and purse. "I'll probably catch some terrible tropical disease and end up spending the entire vacation desperately ill," she predicted direly.

CHAPTER 2

*N*eal Byrne turned the bottle of water in his hands. Even this early, the heat and humidity left a cloud of condensation on the cold surface. He traced a pattern in it until he recognized the tattoo he was drawing and wiped it entirely out with his thumb.

That wasn't his life anymore.

He lifted his gaze and looked out over the green lawn and tropical foliage. His life now seemed equally absurd: a gazelle cropped at the grass nearby, ignoring him.

"Aren't we a pair," Neal told her.

Neal made a point of searching her out every morning, offering an anchor of humanity and familiarity from which to start her path back to civilization.

The gazelle had been imprisoned in Beehag's horrific shifter collection for longer than Neal had been there, and he had spent ten wretched years in that place. Freedom and speech still felt strange to him and clearly the gazelle had not yet acclimated either, never shifting to her human form, barely tolerating bipedal presence at all.

Neal, by contrast, now refused his own animal form.

Beehag had forced him to be a red-maned wolf in his zoo, for his entertainment. Neal rejected everything that reminded him of that captivity, burying his wolf so deeply now that he couldn't even hear its voice.

Mostly, he was ignored by the gazelle, his rusty conversation entirely one-sided, but he noticed that she came to this part of the grounds every morning, despite having the run of the island, so he continued to return, too.

"Breakfast is out," a cheerful voice announced. The gazelle moved swiftly to the far end of the lawn, ears twitching in alarm, then put her head down to graze again.

Breck, head waiter of the resort and a leopard shifter, came over to the bench where Neal sat, holding a heaped plate of food from the gourmet buffet, followed by Graham, the groundskeeper. Although the staff was allowed free rein of the resort food, they were not permitted to eat it in the guest dining room. The picnic table where Neal met the gazelle every morning had become a gathering place for a few of the staff, and somehow, despite his attempts to remain aloof, Neal had found a new place to belong in their motley ranks. He did whatever odd tasks were assigned to him and used his free time to work at getting the remaining survivors of Beehag's prison back to their lost families.

Strangely, he could face helping them, but not the idea of returning to his own life.

Graham, a lion shifter, sat down opposite him, grunting wordlessly in what Neal now recognized was a greeting.

Breck filled any conversational space left by the surly landscaper and the quiet refugee with practiced ease. "Today would be a great day to avoid Scarlet," he advised needlessly.

Scarlet, the owner of the resort, had a short temper and a ferocious will. Neal knew that he and the other rescued shifters were there by her generosity and was grateful for it, but kept out of her way as much as possible. He didn't want a reminder that he and the others were costing her money to keep, and he couldn't tell her when he was going to be ready to leave the insulated island.

Breck continued despite the stony silence. "I guess there are some legal inheritance issues with the island property now that our friend Beehag is out of the picture, and there may be some uncertainty for the long-term lease of Shifting Sands," he said conversationally, eating a slice of quiche with a fork. "We're over capacity in free guests, and under in paid." He paused, giving an eloquent shrug and nod at Neal. "No one blames you, but you might want to keep out of her way, just the same."

Neal shrugged back and Graham put an entire slice of the quiche in his mouth.

"What needs done today?" Neal asked, snagging an extra slice of the egg pie from Breck's plate over his feigned protest.

Neal hated any reminder of Scarlet's charity and avoided the dining hall whenever possible. It hadn't escaped his notice that Breck's breakfast plate had doubled in size since they first started meeting at this table, but none of them actually mentioned it out loud. Neal pretended he was stealing Breck's food, Breck pretended he was bothered by it, and Graham studiously ignored it all.

"There aren't enough guests to need any extra wait-staff," Breck answered him.

Neal was glad. While he could feign good manners and keep from swearing, he didn't fit in at the restaurant any better than the waitstaff uniforms fit him.

"Always weeds," Graham growled. "And the pool needs to be scraped."

"I'll do the pool," Neal volunteered. The last time he

had tried to help Graham with the gardening, he'd pulled up a domesticated vine, and he actually thought for several moments that the lion shifter was going to deck him over the mistake. He could probably hold his own against the groundskeeper, but he didn't want to find out.

After eating half of Breck's plate of food and listening the resort gossip, Neal stood up.

"I want to get the pool done before it gets too hot," he said.

"Catch you this afternoon," Breck said cheerfully.

Graham grunted.

The gazelle gave him a long soulful look from across the lawn, then wandered away through the brush.

Neal shed his resort shirt at the supply shed and exchanged it for the long-handed algae scraper and net he would need for the pool job. It wasn't glamorous labor, but it was physically intense and the sun on the pool deck would be brutal later in the day. It was good work, requiring attention, and Neal tackled it with all of the frustration and bitterness that boiled in his blood.

He was about halfway down the first side of the enormous pool, sweating profusely and enjoying the burn in his muscles, when he felt his red maned wolf stir suddenly, deep inside.

"*No,*" he said ferociously out loud, and he scraped at the tile more vigorously, the thin velvet of algae dissolving before his assault.

To his surprise, his wolf growled back, the urgency of his message too keen to back down.

Without wanting to, Neal looked up and found his head swiveling to the deck by the bar.

A figure stood looking out over the bar deck, and Neal was grateful that she hadn't noticed him yet, because he had to stare for a long moment.

She was the kind of pale that only very new visitors to the resort could be, with mousy blonde hair and big, terrified eyes under a wide-brimmed hat. She had a bag clutched to her chest and one sandal-clad foot was tucked behind the other, rubbing nervously at the opposite heel.

She had the timid, diffident body posture that usually made Neal want to roll his eyes and avoid a person, but there was something about her—something more than the incredibly sexy curves that she seemed be trying to hide. Something that inflamed his senses and made him acutely aware of every pore of her perfect skin.

She's ours, his wolf told him firmly, and the conviction was so deep and determined that Neal had to turn away to fight it back down.

The worst part was, Neal knew he was right. That woman—that gorgeous, petrified woman—was his mate. He unexpectedly knew the iron core of her soul and could taste the gentle sweetness of her mouth. He wanted to kiss her, more than any urge he'd ever had, and was already fantasizing the feel of her pale skin under his calloused fingers.

He drew himself up short.

There was no way in hell he was going to subject her to himself. He was too broken from his years of captivity, his control of himself was too tenuous. It would be best for everyone just to keep his distance.

He shouldered the pool tools and headed the long way around the water to the service entrance where he would be able to avoid looking back at her. *Don't meet her eyes*, he told himself. *Don't let her see you.*

No matter how much he longed to.

CHAPTER 3

*M*ary had never felt so alone.

The owner of the resort, Scarlet Stanson, had been outwardly welcoming, but Mary couldn't help but feel like a grubby child in her tidy office. A grubby child who didn't quite measure up to the incredibly high standards of Shifting Sands Resort.

She had never been somewhere so polished and gorgeous. Even the walkways and steps were beautifully tiled, every plant groomed into the perfect shape. The buildings were all meticulous, even the ones clearly under renovation were well-contained and neater than a construction site had any business being.

Alice would have loved it here, Mary kept thinking, and she longed for her friend's boisterous company. Alice would never have felt intimidated by Scarlet's flawless hair.

But Alice had gotten chicken pox, of all the ridiculous things, and been forced to stay home. After everything she'd done to convince Mary that this would be the holiday she needed, Alice hadn't even been able to go. Getting on the plane by herself had been the bravest thing that Mary had ever done. At first, she'd considered refusing, but Alice had been adamant. *At least one of us is getting some enjoyment out of the cottage I booked, so you'd better go, or I'll come back as a ghost and haunt you for the rest of your days!*

Even pointing out that chicken pox was rarely fatal hadn't put a dent in Alice's fervor, and in the end Mary had reluctantly decided she didn't have a choice.

Clutching her map and her bag, already regretting her decision to come alone, Mary decided to go to the pool first, to familiarize herself with the layout and see if it was really as impressive as the photographs had made it out to be. The closest access was through the bar, but when she stepped out onto the deck, the ocean view arrested her before she even noticed the pool.

Even as far away as it was, she could feel the magnetic power of water and hear the waves crashing on the reef that protected the bay. There was a scent and a quality to the air that she'd never experienced before, salty and metallic and *alive*.

She couldn't even imagine swimming in such a thing. It was full of power and secrets and strength. Her shifter-self felt strangely stronger here, more alive than it had ever been in the sleepy little town of Lakefield.

She turned her gaze to the pool, but before she saw the pool itself, she saw *him*.

He was looking away, in that swift way people do when they've just caught themselves staring, but Mary was sure it couldn't have been *her* that he was staring at.

He had a shock of short red hair, mussed from exertion, and a stubborn tan you rarely found on redheads. That tan spread over muscles unlike any Mary had ever seen before outside of sports magazines. He had wide shoulders knotted with strength and arms like small trees. His narrow hips were clad in utilitarian shorts and his feet were bare. As Mary tried not to stare and failed, he gathered up his pool cleaning equipment and stalked away, never turning his face to her.

His exit left Mary feeling lonelier and full of longing than ever. Within her, something awoke and uncoiled. Part of her wanted to drop her bag and run down the stairs after the gorgeous man, even as the practical part said that was ridiculous and she was just reacting to a stunning male specimen after a dry spell in her life. It wasn't like she *really* believed any of that nonsense about fated mates or destined love.

Mary sighed and finally looked at the pool.

It was long enough for laps in either direction, with two waterfalls cascading from small pools at the bar deck she stood on down to the water level of the pool. Palm trees lined both sides, leaning over massive boulders on the left and spaced along a wide walkway to the right. At the far end, the poolside deck was peppered with chairs and umbrellas and guests lying out in the sun. Beyond that lay the terrifying ocean. Elevation hid the beach from her, but Mary guessed it lay below the pool deck; the island was quite steep.

No one was currently swimming in the pool and the last agitation from the gorgeous pool cleaner's efforts had already died down. Only the ripples from the water features disturbed the surface. Mary could see the deep bottom, the curved steps at the far end, and the globes of the lights that would illuminate the water at night. Would it be too scary to swim at night? It didn't look like there were very many lights around the pool.

As hot as the day was, the water looked deliciously cool. It was supposed to be unheated, something that Mary had been hesitant about until she stepped off the plane into the tropical Costa Rican heat.

A swim would have to wait, though, because she wasn't planning to change into her swimsuit here on the pool deck, no matter what kind of lax clothing rules there were at this strange place.

Mary took the exit that her map indicated was closest to her cottage and followed a pristine white gravel path to a charming little house with a beautiful private deck. It looked like something straight out of a tropical-themed issue of Good Housekeeping. Mary had another pang of loneliness and nervousness glancing at the bed in the empty second bedroom. If Alice were with her, she probably would have chased down the hunky man by the pool and insisted that he give them a tour of the resort and meet them for drinks afterwards.

For some reason, she could not get the picture of him out of her mind. Not just his juicy shoulders and ripped body, but the planes of the cheek that she'd gotten a glimpse of, the ruffle of his hair, and... something about the way he held himself. Like he hurt. Maybe not physically, but...

Mary ached for him, then shook her head and changed into her swimsuit. She didn't even *know* him!

CHAPTER 4

"*A*ren't there any jobs that aren't at the center of the resort?" Neal asked, trying not to sound whiny or ungrateful, though he honestly felt both. "Isn't there an urgent need to clear vines off the waterfall hiking trail or wrestle sharks on the other side of the island or something?"

It had been getting harder and harder to dodge the blonde with the big hat over the last few days. He always knew where she was, and he was beginning to suspect that she was actively looking for him. Already he had feigned illness to avoid being assigned to the waitstaff as she was heading for the restaurant and had shirked pool deck cleanup twice when he realized that she was there swimming laps. He knew he was in danger of being perceived as a slacker and avoiding Scarlet as well was turning navigation of the resort into a complicated challenge.

Travis, looking over the duty roster, made a noise of sympathy. "Unless you're secretly a certified electrician…?"

Neal had to shrug a negative.

"There's nothing left to do at the cottages I'm renovating until the wiring is in, and I won't be able to start in on that until tomorrow." Travis, a lynx shifter from Alaska, was apparently certified in every kind of construction and also drove the boat that ferried guests from the mainland when they didn't come by small plane to the airport on the other side of the island.

Neal was certified in plenty of things, but he wasn't sure how being able to set explosives and shoot the wings off a fly from a mile away would make him useful at the resort. He'd earned EMT certification, but that didn't distinguish him from the lifeguard, and any certification he had would be expired after ten years of captivity anyway.

"You could take the day off," Tex suggested with the drawl that explained his nickname.

Neal stared at the bear shifter bartender as if he'd grown horns.

"If you don't want to, *I* could use the day off," Bastian said with unexpectedly wistfulness. Neal was a little surprised—he knew Bastian liked to do his lifeguard duties in dragon-form, but Neal realized he had no idea what else he liked to do, or why he might need a day off to do it. As far as Neal knew, he spent all day, every day, on the beach, with one jeweled eye on the pool.

"I'm not qualified as a lifeguard," Neal said regretfully. The woman who was haunting him seemed to avoid the beach, staying to the pool and well-groomed grounds around the guest center. The beach might actually be a safe place to spend the day.

"Want to be?" the dragon offered cheerfully. "Costa Rican requirements aren't all that difficult, and I'm autho-rized to approve you if you can pass the swimming test and listen to me drone a bit in a crash course about waterfront safety."

Neal accepted gratefully; his swimming skills were strong, so passing didn't concern him.

Much later, gasping for breath, lungs burning and eyes watering from the saltwater, Neal decided that he should have been concerned.

"Nice work," Bastian said without irony after the final lap. "I'll have Scarlet print you up a temporary certificate in her office, and you can take over lifeguard duties for the afternoon."

Neal clung to the edge of the dock for a moment before heaving himself up. "I passed?"

"Oh," Bastian said, slightly sheepish. "A while ago, yes. I just wanted to see how much you could do."

"I'm going to kill you when I can move my arms again," Neal said, cheerfully exhausted. On the upside, he hadn't thought about his mate once since the test had started.

He would have gone straight for the buffet, starving from the exertion, but his unerring compass for the woman's location told him that she was already there, so Neal limped himself to the staff quarters instead, and collapsed on the picnic table in the sun.

Just as he was considering sneaking into the kitchen and braving Chef's wrath to steal food directly, Breck appeared with a plate of food and a bottle of water. He didn't even feign bringing it for himself but put it right in front of Neal.

"Well done on Bastian's brutal test!" he said admiringly, fanning himself.

"Saw that, did you?" Neal figured Breck was just teasing him. The head waiter flirted with everyone, men and women alike, but no one seemed to take it very seriously.

"The two of you, swimming around at the dock in

those little shorts? Wouldn't have missed it for the world!" Breck winked and Neal was too tired to glare back.

"Congratulations on your certificate," a gentle voice interrupted them.

Neal sat up respectfully in his seat and stopped shoveling food into his face. "You heard about that, too, Mrs. Atheson?" he asked sheepishly, looking at the petite older woman who was smiling at him.

"It was a perfectly *lovely* show," the ocelot shifter said with a saucy wink. "A number of us were watching from the pool deck."

Neal blushed.

Then he realized that she was holding a small piece of luggage.

"You're leaving," he said in surprise.

Like the gazelle, she had spent longer in Beehag's zoo than Neal had, and she had very few belongings.

"Amber and Tony have bought a house in Maryland that has a mother-in-law apartment attached, and they're anxious to have me move back to the States. Tony has gotten the visa all sorted through his agency." She settled beside him on the picnic bench. "There are no more leads here to help me find my husband, and let's be honest, if he's even alive at all, it's unlikely he will come back to this island. If he does, Scarlet assures me she will send him my way."

"She will." Neal could say that with conviction. However temperamental Scarlet was, she was deeply honorable.

"More than that, I'm finally ready to be back out in the world," Mrs. Atheson said softly.

I'm not, Neal couldn't say out loud.

He only leaned over and let Mrs. Atheson enfold him in a motherly hug.

"Thank you for all of your help," she said. Near his ear, she whispered, "You'll be ready sooner than you think, too."

Neal gave her an extra squeeze and insisted on carrying her light bag up the last steps and out the resort entrance to where a Jeep was waiting to take her to the airstrip on the other side of the island.

Neal struggled with her departure, keeping a brave face over the stumbling uncertainty that he felt. Breck made no bones about crying as he hugged her goodbye, but Neal kept a stony face, not wanting to admit the empty hole that remained as the Jeep sped away. It was a gap made more keen by the impossible nearness and imposed distance he was keeping from his mate.

She was so close, he sensed, and part of him wanted to find solace in her touch. The rest of him wanted to save her from his poisoned brokenness.

CHAPTER 5

*T*he pool alone was worth the grueling journey, Mary decided again. She had come to that conclusion her very first day at Shifting Sands, and every morning discovered it all over again.

The frightening foreign airport, the tiny cramped airplane ride, and the terrifying winding drive from the airstrip were all small payment for the delicious cool laps she could do in the stunning pool. Very rarely did she have to share the water with others, who seemed to prefer the beach or lying in the sun on the deck as humans or animals. There were never any raucous children running around to spoil the peace. The space was long enough that she could lose herself in the stroke and kick, and feel graceful and athletic, as she never did out of the water.

The palm trees made dappled shade that she could rest in at the edges, or she could choose a sunny spot to tip her face up to.

She got a massage the first day, and a pedicure and a haircut the second. The Spanish-accented woman who ran the spa, Lydia, offered to groom her in animal form, but Mary demurred; that felt a little intimate.

The staff as a whole was welcoming and friendly. The few times she'd seen Scarlet, the woman had gravely asked if she was enjoying herself, which Mary could always answer with enthusiastic affirmative. The handsome head waiter, Breck, flirted with her unexpectedly, skirting the very edge of too much attention to keep it easy-going rather than outrageous. Her housekeeper even apologized for the unseasonable amount of rain they were having, as if it were something they could control.

If it hadn't been for the mysterious pool cleaner who haunted her thoughts, Mary would have believed it was an absolutely perfect vacation.

After the first glimpse of him, she hadn't been able to erase him from her mind.

She couldn't quite stop herself from imagining climbing out of the pool and into the arms of the mysterious man she'd seen cleaning the pool. As she did her lazy laps, she lost herself in the idea of those strong arms wrapped around her, her mouth finding his as they slipped under the salty ripples of the water.

She continued to spot him nearly every day, always hurrying away from her with a loping stride that she wouldn't have been able to catch if she'd tried. She was beginning to think that he was avoiding her. She suspected that he felt the same pull she did, but sensed it made him uncomfortable, rather than intrigued. She still couldn't quite bring herself to believe it, but more than once she'd caught herself wondering, *Could mates be a real thing after all?*

It grieved her to think she was causing him discomfort, and she wanted to catch him, to say that she would never make him sad or unhappy, and that she was sorry she seemed to be causing him distress. She wondered if there was something she could do to help him—she could still feel the pain that crackled off of him.

She felt like one of her own students, enslaved to her own crazy adolescent hormones, and she could not stop fantasizing about him: about what it would feel like to kiss him, to slide her hands over his shoulders, to feel the weight of him on her when she lay in her wide bed.

Finally, three days into her vacation, she spotted him across the pool deck.

"Oh!" she said out loud, stopping in her tracks.

There he was, close as life, bending over a bucket of supplies by one of the lounge chairs; Mary would know his silhouette and the burst of his red hair anywhere, and she had a moment of near-terror.

She knew that he would find an excuse to leave at any moment, and it would have been easy to let him go. At any other time in her life, she would simply have lingered in the doorway a little longer and watched him escape from her again.

But she was here, being brave and courageous, in a foreign country by herself. She wasn't sure if it was the hot weather or the glamour of Shifting Sands itself, but she even felt like a more powerful shifter here; all of her senses were sharper than they'd ever been, and they were all focused entirely on *him*.

She gathered all of her resolve and walked decisively across the tiled deck, weaving around the chairs and tables on the deck without removing her eyes from him.

"I'm sorry," she said automatically, when she was finally at his side and, abruptly, the bravery that had carried her across the deck vanished. She was left feeling like a stammering fool, awkward and unappealing in her plain blue swimsuit and cheap flip-flops. She was keenly aware of the few other guests enjoying the late afternoon sunshine on the deck, including a sleek, manicured woman wearing almost nothing and the bartender who was strumming a guitar at the bar behind her.

"I'm sorry," she repeated. "I don't mean to interrupt you, it's just that... I... ah..."

He was looking at her with hazel eyes like saucers, as unable to look away as Mary was. He was more gorgeous up close than he was fleeing from her across a pool deck or down a path, built like an athlete, with wide shoulders under his resort uniform shirt and narrow hips in khaki shorts. Agile hands were clenched, white-knuckled, around the bucket handle.

All of the hurt she had sensed from him was there, intense and bone-deep.

"Oh!" she said in wonder. "You feel it too!"

Because, laid over the hurt was something else—the heat and lust and a depth of connection that Mary had never even dared to hope for.

This is our mate, her deer told her with no hesitation, pleased and excited.

Mary had always wondered if a destined mate could be real and hadn't dared to hope that her odd attraction to this stranger could be such a thing.

Meeting his eyes dissolved any doubt she might have had. She could feel a resonance between them that defied description. Magic seemed to crackle around them, and she reached out an automatic hand to touch him in wonder.

He flinched away, and the spell shattered.

His face shuttered, settling into an off-putting scowl, and he stood, towering over her. "I don't know what you're talking about," he snarled at her.

Then he turned on his heel and walked away, leaving Mary feeling utterly lost.

CHAPTER 6

*R*ejecting her was the hardest thing that Neal had ever done—watching her heart break into little pieces while he denied the pull of their mating bond was like being shot. He was worthless, terrible, the worst kind of jerk... and the biggest coward that had ever had the misfortune to walk the face of the earth on two legs and on four.

He sank down onto a picnic table seat, steepling his hands on the back of his head. He wanted to tear something into pieces, or burn something to the ground. His mate was hurting, and he couldn't do anything to protect her, because *he* was the one who had caused it.

What had *happened* to him?

At one point, he'd been part of one of the most elite teams in the military, a sharpshooter and explosives expert with a reputation for being fearless and unstoppable. He'd been confident with women and complicated missions alike.

Now he was reduced to doing odd jobs at a fancy tropical resort and failing even at that: fearful, prickly and unfit for any friendship, let alone the company of his own destined mate.

Why did she have to come here, of all places? Couldn't they just have been another unlucky couple who never had the grace to meet?

Something tickled at the side of his neck, a whuffle of air and short whiskers, and Neal snapped around to find that the gazelle had come closer to him than he had ever seen her, big eyes and mobile ears all focused on him. Familiar tension ran in every muscle along her neck. He saw that same tension in the mirror every day.

"There was a time you wouldn't have been able to get within a hundred yards without me noticing you," he told her dryly, letting his fists fall open with effort.

The gazelle only blinked in reply. There was a time she wouldn't have come within a hundred yards at all.

"I'm pretty awful at being a human being anymore," he continued conversationally. "Maybe I should have stayed in Beehag's zoo."

The gazelle snorted and Neal swore she actually rolled her eyes.

Even suggesting it sarcastically gave Neal chills and sweats. He could still remember the cold feeling of the bars as he pressed against them and the hot electric shocks that had been applied when he had tried to stubbornly remain in human form. He groaned and rolled his shoulders back.

"She's better off without me," he said firmly. "She doesn't need the mess that is me in her life."

Ears twitching, the gazelle dropped her nose to the hand that Neal had made into a fist again and touched it tentatively.

As far as Neal was aware, it was the first touch that she had tolerated since her release, and the honor of that penetrated his shell of self-pity.

He held his breath, not wanting to startle her away again.

"Neal."

The moment was broken by a completely unwelcome voice, and the gazelle was bounding away before he could even move to reassure her.

He was all prickles and anger and fury as he turned to face Scarlet.

The resort owner was dressed in a pressed khaki suit with a skirt to her knees and her hair, redder even than his own, was pulled in a tidy bun at the back of her head.

"You missed another staff meeting," she said, not sitting.

He stood up, not comfortable being shorter than her, but towering over her by half a foot did not seem to intimidate her in the least. She only gave him a flinty emerald gaze, her chin uplifted as she waited for his explanation.

"I'm sorry," he ground out, knowing he sounded anything but.

Unexpectedly, her face softened to pity and she gestured him to sit as she did the same, with all the confidence of a queen. Neal stubbornly remained standing, not wanting her pity.

"Neal," Scarlet said more gently. "You came to us under unusual circumstances, and you've worked hard to make yourself a place here."

Until this last week, Neal would have agreed with her. He didn't give her the satisfaction of a response.

"You've also been invaluable with the other refugees from Beehag's estate," Scarlet observed, which wasn't something that Neal had realized she knew about.

He continued to offer only the stoniest of faces.

"Most of them have been reunited with family and returned home now," Scarlet went on, unfazed by his lack of response. "And I'm not blind to the fact that you've played a large role in preparing them for that transition." She gestured across the lawn, and Neal noticed that the gazelle had not fled far. She was still standing in earshot, head upright.

"There's a limit, though." Scarlet's voice took on an edge. "To my patience, and to yours."

Neal braced himself.

"Shifting Sands is not your home," she said, like ice.

Neal almost had to sit. She was... firing him? Kicking him out? His first reaction was anger, followed by a drifting uncertainty and mournful feeling that she was right to. He buried it all behind an unwavering scowl, as deeply as he was burying his own wolf.

"You cannot make yourself whole here," she said, with all the haughtiness of a queen. "And I don't have the resources to pander to your cowardice forever."

Cowardice? No one had ever accused him of that—no one had ever dared, and Neal was not sure how to take it from the manicured woman who sat before him with her hands folded easily in her lap.

"I'm happy to remove myself," he said with automatic defensiveness, but even as he said it, he wasn't sure how he would do so. He had no money, no identity—he had undoubtedly been given up for dead by now, by his team and by his family.

A piece of paper seemed to materialize in Scarlet's hand as she outstretched it to him.

He took it, but didn't look at it, not wanting to show weakness by breaking their eye contact first.

"Those are the current contact numbers of the members of your unit," Scarlet said.

Neal had to look at the paper in shock then, nearly dropping it. How did she even know about them? He had been vague about his life before Beehag's zoo and discouraged discussion about it vehemently.

"There's also the number for your niece," Scarlet went on, as if she hadn't noticed his utter and complete shock. "I thought that might be easier than contacting your sister directly."

She stood and brushed off her skirt, looking as cool as could be in the muggy afternoon heat.

"I don't need your charity," Neal lied to her, crumpling the paper into his pocket as if he didn't care.

"Of course not," Scarlet replied. "I haven't given you any. But as a temporary member of my staff, please be reminded that I will not tolerate rudeness to my guests."

It made Neal feel prickly and angry and ashamed to think that she knew about *that*, too.

She left before he could find an appropriate rebuttal.

He was diving into his pocket before she was even out of sight, smoothing out the page and staring at the numbers as if they were ciphers to the locks in his head.

There was a landline in the staff building, but he wasn't sure he was ready to make any of the calls.

But there *was* one call he was ready to make.

CHAPTER 7

$\mathcal{M}$ary stared at the magazine article until the words stopped making sense.

She couldn't even have said what it was about; every effort to read seemed to drift off into daydreaming about the red-haired pool cleaner. She couldn't stop thinking about the way his bare muscles gleamed in the tropical sun, and she kept remembering the frightful snarl as he pushed away from her.

She looked down at her skin, still pale against her utilitarian blue one-piece, and frowned at the curve of her hips and legs, resisting the impulse to pull a towel over herself. Maybe he was disappointed by her. Maybe he didn't want her for a mate. Maybe he wanted one of the taller, richer, tanned guests, in their tiny two-pieces and sparkly high heels.

Mary shook her head and put the magazine down. As familiar as the idea was, she couldn't bring herself to entirely believe it. Not after seeing into his eyes. He had wanted her as badly as she wanted him.

"You need a drink, honey?"

Settling into the deck chair beside her was a woman so enormous that Mary half-expected the chair to collapse, rolls of golden flesh barely contained by a fluttery, bright orange bikini.

"I'm sorry?"

"A drink," the woman suggested, lowering her sunglasses to peer at Mary with brilliant violet eyes. "Tex makes a margarita to die for."

"Oh, I couldn't," Mary said, flustered by the woman's intense gaze. "I don't really... I wouldn't..."

That earned her a tolerant smile. "Well, *I'm* ordering one," the woman chuckled, and she waved an imperious arm in the air towards the bar deck above them that made her chair creak in protest.

She must have caught someone's eyes, and her order must have been expected, because very shortly, Mary heard the distant whine of a blender over the waves crashing on the beach below them.

"I'm Magnolia, darling." The woman's offered hand was perfectly manicured, and her handshake was firm but gentle. Several jeweled rings decked her thick fingers.

"Mary," she answered, bemused, wondering what Magnolia took from her own handshake.

"You're in a knot about something," Magnolia suggested casually, leaning back into her chair and dropping her sunglasses back into place.

Mary had braced herself for casual conversation and was prepared to reveal the unstimulating truth that she was a math teacher from the Midwest and then talk about the lovely weather.

Magnolia's observation caught her by surprise and tears pricked at her eyes. She ducked her head and hoped that her hat's wide brim would keep her face from Magnolia's view as she muttered, "It's nothing..."

She was not so lucky. When Magnolia's chair groaned like a dying hyena, Mary looked up in alarm to find that the other woman had swung her legs around and was sitting up with both hands offered this time.

Mary mirrored her, letting Magnolia enfold her pale fingers in her larger ones. "Do you believe in destined mates?" she asked hesitantly, not daring to look up.

"Yes," Magnolia said without any hesitation of her own. There was a richness to the single word, a depth of understanding that Mary hadn't realized she was hoping for.

"What if he... doesn't want me?"

Magnolia's laughter made Mary lift her head.

"It doesn't work like that, sweetie." Magnolia said it very gently, as if to a small child. "You know that, don't you?"

"I don't understand, then," Mary said, with all the frustration that had been building in her. "Why does he keep running away?"

"Finding your mate doesn't always mean your fairy tale happy ending is at hand. Sometimes you need a little patience."

Mary thought there was a note of sadness in her voice, and maybe a hint of dry amusement.

"His name is Neal," Magnolia told her, and it took Mary's breath away to hear it.

It was such an odd sensation, almost like she recognized the name, but not quite.

A server appeared beside them, and Mary looked up to find that she was holding a tray with two margaritas.

"Oh goodness," Magnolia said, releasing Mary's hand and taking one of the glasses. "I can't drink two of these."

Mary suspected that Magnolia would have been able to

down a dozen of them without effect, but she took the
other anyway, unexpectedly eager for it.

"Tell me more," she begged, once the server was gone
again.

"Only Neal can tell you the whole story," Magnolia
said, settling back into her chair again. "But I'll tell you
what I know."

CHAPTER 8

$\mathcal{N}$eal pulled at the collar of the shirt.

It was a far cry from the well-tailored dress uniform he had attended military functions in, but it was more appropriate than the resort polo shirt and khaki shorts he usually wore. Travis, the resort handyman, had done an admirable job of fitting one of the waitstaff uniforms to him, as long as you didn't look too closely at the mismatched fabric under the arms.

"Don't pluck at it," Travis scolded, swatting at Neal's hands and adjusting the collar of the coat himself.

"Are you sure you aren't going to need backup, to see that you don't chicken out?" Breck added.

Neal bit back the automatic offense at the insult. Breck meant well and was only trying to be helpful. It wasn't like Neal didn't deserve a little ribbing for being a coward.

Tex strummed some dire chords on his guitar, sprawled across Neal's bed. "Do you want some musical backup?" he offered. "Women love to be serenaded."

Breck scoffed. "Sure, put her in the mood with a ditty about getting hit by a pickup and shooting a dog."

"I know some love songs," Tex chuckled, but the tune he played was anything but.

"Sad love songs don't count," Bastian said, shaking his head.

"You kidding?" Travis mocked. "Have you ever watched a chick flick? Girls love to cry."

Neal was not sure when this whole thing had turned into such a public affair, but his room in the staff housing was stuffed with supposedly helpful staff. Bastian was draped across his desk chair, and Travis was grinning at him from the footlocker.

"She's a deer, remember, so avoid predator jokes," Bastian suggested helpfully. Breck had risked his job and his skin by snooping into Scarlet's office for Mary's information and cottage number, to Neal's chagrin and gratitude when he found out.

"You should probably avoid *any* jokes," Tex added dryly. "You're not very good at them."

A determined knock at the door stilled the merriment of the room, and Breck opened it.

"Why, Graham," he said in mischievous delight. "I've been waiting for this day since I laid eyes on your gorgeous face!"

Graham scowled back and shoved past him to put the armload of flowers he was holding into Neal's hands.

The staff voiced their appreciation of the gesture with whistles of awe and murmurs of surprise; Graham was notoriously stingy about cutting his precious blooms. The staff liked to tell a story about him nearly coming to blows with Chef over using cut flowers in the dining hall without his blessing.

Neal took the bouquet with the same gravity that Graham had offered it. "Thanks, man," he said gruffly. He said it generally to the room and didn't wait to see their reactions, but simply marched out the door decisively, because he knew that if he lingered much longer, he would do exactly as Breck had suggested and completely chicken out.

The march across the resort grounds was as difficult as any mission behind enemy lines that Neal had undertaken, and he was sweating by the time he reached Mary's cottage, despite the cool evening drizzle and the downhill path. He was grateful for the shroud of darkness, but he paused when he reached her door, suddenly not sure if he should knock. Possibly it was too late for his visit. Maybe this was something better saved for daylight and safer times.

For a long moment, he hesitated. But then, gritting his teeth, he realized that this was something he *had* to do.

Making his hand land on the door was harder than any shot he'd ever taken and sounded just as loud to his ears.

A second knock was not going to happen, but fortunately, the door sprang open as if he had been expected, and he was frozen as Mary looked up at him, standing in a pale nightgown in the doorway, every curve a promise of forever.

"You came," she breathed, and Neal dropped the bouquet to catch her as she hurled herself into his arms.

CHAPTER 9

*M*ary's sense of where Neal was had never been terribly specific—she often found herself at a staff gate with the general idea that he was 'that way,' but she couldn't break the sanctity of a staff-only sign, too aware of how precious the privacy of her own teacher's lounge was.

So when she had a sudden awareness of his proximity, lying on her bed with a magazine, waiting for elusive sleep, it was a shock.

I should be wearing something sexier, she thought with chagrin. Her nightgown was old-fashioned and modest, something more appropriate for sleepovers with a girl-friend than a midnight tryst with her reluctant mate.

She was off her bed and halfway to the dresser to inspect her boring lingerie for anything less prudish than 'strictly utilitarian' when the knock came, and she couldn't keep herself from bounding across the room to fling open the door.

She ought to use a subtle touch, she reminded herself.

If she was too forward, he might flee again; she needed to be the perfect combination of reserved and gentle.

But when she saw him, with that shock of short hair bleached of its red in the pale porch light, that handsome face a mix of longing and regret, all she could say do was squeak, "You came!" and throw herself at him.

Not your most restrained moment, she told herself.

He had no choice but to catch her, but instead of setting her sensibly on her feet, as Mary was expecting, he wrapped his arms around her tightly and pressed his mouth to hers.

Mary had never been kissed like Neal kissed her. She hadn't known a kiss like that was possible. It was deep and involved the entire mouth, and she was keenly aware of being pulled against him. The pressure of his body against hers was irresistible, sending her into a tailspin of desire and lust.

She had her arms around his neck, pulling herself deeper into the kiss, craving the closeness of his body and the honeyed salt of his mouth. She'd read of kisses described as electric, but she'd always thought it was a foolish expression—until now, with Neal sending shocks of pleasure to her toes and her fingertips. Her entire body was more alive than she had ever imagined it could be.

Her earlier fears were laughable now, her doubts that he may not desire her swept away in the way that he held her, cradling her at the small of her back and the base of her neck; the way he kissed her; and the most undeniable expression of lust that was pressing against her through his pants.

She was dizzy and lightheaded when he finally released her lips, and she gave a sigh of loss even as she gasped for breath.

"Can you forgive me?" he asked her, voice gruff and low.

Mary blinked at him. The kiss left her feeling confused and filled with head-spinning need. Did he want forgiveness for stopping the kiss? "Forgive you for what?"

His laugh was hesitant, like he didn't do it often. "I've been avoiding you. I told you I didn't know what you meant when you finally talked to me. I was a jerk. I was..."

Mary stopped him with a finger on his mouth. It was strange to feel his lips with her fingers. "I forgive you," she said simply.

"I should explain," he said reluctantly, and Mary could have drowned in the sorrow in those eyes.

"You don't have to," she said gently.

Neal stared back. Mary could feel the hesitation in his hands and the muscles of his body.

"I want to help you," she explained. "I want to know what happened to you. But you don't have to tell me until you're really ready. I know who *you* are. I know what you are to *me*."

He gave a great sigh of his own. His gaze softened, and Mary could feel some of his tension ease.

Not the important tension, though, and when he bent to kiss her again, she pressed herself against him like a cat in heat, unable to resist the demands of her own body.

He kissed her again, as her lips had been longing for, no less urgently than the first time, and she fumbled at his jacket buttons, desperate to put her hands against his skin.

They had to break the kiss to shimmy out of clothing, and Mary regretted her simple nightgown not because it wasn't sexy enough—slipping it off was a whisper of sensuality that she'd never expected—but because there weren't enough layers to it. She hadn't anticipated how much fun it would be to undress another person, or how exciting it was to peel through clothing to find the skin beneath.

Once her nightdress was off, Mary paused, and Neal stared for a long, mesmerized moment, holding the thin cotton garment in his big hands. The night air chilled goosebumps onto her flesh despite feeling flushed and hot. Neal gave a groan before tossing the gown to the floor and crushing her back to him for another of their long, deep kisses.

"It's not fair!" she laughed at him when her mouth was free. "I have so much clothing still to get through."

Neal was as impatient with it as she was, and the task was hastened: tie, shirt, and undershirt thrown aside with zeal. His scuffed shoes were wrenched off without untying and the pants were shimmied off to the floor until they both stood in only underwear.

Mary could not keep herself from staring. His briefs did nothing to hide his impressive desire for her, and she wondered if her inescapable dampness showed on her simple cotton underthings.

They were at the door of her bedroom now, and the sounds of the room were the unending insects of the tropical night, the tapping of rain on the roof, and their own breath, ragged and eager.

"Do come in," Mary said at last, feeling suddenly shy.

CHAPTER 10

*N*eal felt as if he'd won some kind of lottery, and he mistrusted his luck, even while Mary's earthy, curvy beauty stunned him into silence.

The roundness of her hips, the softness of her shoulders—it wasn't just his maned wolf that Neal had to wrestle down. Everything about her brought out animal lust and desire in him. He had to struggle to keep his urgency in check, fearful of hurting her, of losing control and not treating her with the care and reverence she deserved.

When she invited him into the sanctity of her bedroom, he went willingly and instead of wrestling her down onto the bed the way he wanted to, he sat, and drew her into his lap.

There was no hiding his lust for her, no tempering the physical part of his need, but Neal forced his hands to be slow, and his kisses to her neck were whispers, not the bites he was so tempted to make. He teased around her breasts, lifting them, stroking them, defining their shape and softness, then finally brushing a finger across her nipples and delighting in the deep groan of need she gave.

She squirmed in his lap, driving him mad with the touch against his cock, and he feared he would embarrass himself before they even got out of their underwear.

He didn't realize that he'd frozen, trying to fight down the need that was rising to a fever pitch, until Mary pushed him back on the bed and slipped out of her underwear.

He stayed still while she wrestled him out of his own, lifting his hips to help her.

They both gave a gasp when his erection sprang free, Neal from the sensation of it, Mary in delight, as far as Neal could tell.

Then she was straddling him, drawing down on him, and Neal had to worship her swinging breasts and sweet flesh. She was slick with moisture, and beautifully, impossibly tight around him, each cautious stroke she made bringing him deeper into her eager folds.

Neal let her ride him, drowning in the incredible sensation of her skin and the honeyed smell of her, until he could bear it no longer. He reached up and rolled her over, never decoupling.

Sprawled beneath him, Mary's eyes were soft and glowing in the dim light of her bedside lamp. Her blonde hair tangled over the crisp white pillow like waves, and Neal had to reach out with one hand and trace the shape of her face, already so unexpectedly dear to him.

"I never thought I'd find you," she said softly, and even her voice was intoxicating.

"I never… " Neal couldn't find the words, too overwhelmed by smell and sight and sensation.

He wasn't sure if he had ever stopped moving, but now he was thrusting again, slowly, deliberately. Every movement was carefully controlled. He was painfully afraid of losing control, of losing *her*, and he wasn't prepared for her writhing moan of pleasure as she crested toward orgasm.

"Don't stop," she begged, and Neal could not have if he tried.

Her blissful sound of climax drove Neal out of his mind, and he only became aware again of himself as someone separate from Mary when the urgency merged into release and faded at last into gasping, grasping satisfaction.

His first thought, when he could think again, was for Mary. Had he hurt her?

Her brilliant smile suggested otherwise, and her laughing hands stroked his shoulders in a fashion that Neal wouldn't have expected to be so soothing.

"That was amazing…"

"I'm sorry… I didn't hurt you?" Neal had to know for sure.

"Hurt me?" Mary sounded amazed by the idea. "Are you kidding? Oh, Neal!"

She reached eager arms to wrap around him and kissed him soundly.

The way she said his name was all the reassurance Neal needed, and the way she kissed him made him wonder if she would be interested in a repeat performance. His basic need for her had been slaked, but the touch of her lips on his made him realize that he would be happy for another round.

He let her draw him down for an embrace and buried his face at her neck, breathing in the scent of her hair and her velvety skin.

I'm sorry, he wanted to say. *I'm sorry I'm not the mate you deserve, or the man I ought to be.*

But he could only hold her, and be grateful for her arms around him, and live in the moment for now.

CHAPTER 11

*M*ary was not particularly surprised to wake alone.

The bed was rumpled and the room smelled like sex and surrender.

Mary sighed and sat up.

Morning light was streaming through the big glass doors. Mary could see down to the hypnotic ocean over the tile roofs of the cottages in front of her and hear the rumbling call of it over the morning birds and the ceaseless chirping insects. She slid one of the doors open and was rewarded by a rush of humid air.

It had rained overnight, and the world was covered in jewels of water. It was already warming up, and Mary knew from the past few days that the sun would quickly burn off the lingering fog and evaporate the moisture. By mid-morning, it would be sweltering and blue again, and mid-afternoon there might be more warm showers.

There was a tiny lizard on the railing of the deck, and Mary eyed it skeptically. The first day at the resort, a lizard so close would have sent her scurrying back inside, but she was too wrapped up in thinking of Neal to mind it.

Mary continued to think, vacillating between frustration and warm, lustful memories, as she dressed and showered. She walked in a daze out of her cottage, only to turn in the wrong direction on the path and walk directly into a glittering spiderweb.

The sticky brush of it on her skin, the tickling of it in her hair and on her bare arms was bad enough, but out of the corner of her eye, Mary could see the giant orb of the viciously striped creature, bobbing on its tangled home. Bobbing *towards* her, hairy legs waving aggressively.

Mary screamed, skin crawling and adrenaline spiking, flailing her arms. The web was stickier and stronger than she expected, and the spider moved so quickly that she panicked, screaming again and leaping away.

A figure blocked her path, so looming and terrifying in its silence and menace that Mary barely recognized it as the landscaper before she was shifting out of instinct.

"Mary!"

It was Neal's voice, and it was the only thing that kept her from flinging herself in deer form in a panic through the brush—where there were undoubtedly more spiderwebs waiting to ensnare her.

She stopped in her tracks, quivering.

The landscaper growled at her and then went past. He went from frightful to horrifying as he scooped up the spider from its ruined web, right into his bare hands. "She wouldn't hurt you," he said accusingly, clearly more concerned with the spider than the deer.

Then Neal was there, sprinting over and snarling ferociously, hands balled into fists as he tried to figure out what was threatening Mary.

The surly gardener was the obvious choice and Neal did not hesitate to come roaring to Mary's rescue.

Wait! she tried to call to him through their bond, but he either didn't hear or was too deep in protective rage to notice, lunging for the man holding the spider.

Given his animal growl, Mary expected Neal to shift and was surprised when he didn't.

The gardener dodged with more speed than either she or Neal anticipated and continued to cup the spider protectively in one hand while deflecting Neal's attack with the other.

Neal cornered with the kind of strength and reflexes that could only come from intense training and shifter advantages, snarling and striking at the other man while Mary wailed *Stop!* and Neal didn't seem to hear her.

The landscaper fought only defensively and was hampered by carefully holding his arachnid friend, but still managed to block most of Neal's rain of blows, absorbing the rest with an impressive show of imperviousness. Mary had never seen such combat outside of movies and was stunned by the ferocity and might of Neal's attack.

Finally, she managed to get enough of a hold on herself to shift back to her human form, and she ran forward, knowing she had to try to stop this. "Neal, no! He didn't do anything, it's okay! It wasn't him!"

The look he leveled at her was feral and full of panic but faded abruptly at her words, and he pulled the blow he was landing, letting the momentum of it pull him forwards into a slumping crouch. Mary went to him at once, putting her hands on his shoulders without hesitation. He flinched, then looked up in chagrin. "I'm sorry, Graham."

The gardener wiped away a trail of blood from his mouth and shrugged, looking genuinely unconcerned as he turned to deposit the spider gently onto a branch.

"It was just a spider," Mary explained soothingly. "I walked into a spiderweb and it scared me. That's all that happened. I guess… it was a shifter spider?" She looked at Graham for some confirmation, but he only scowled at her and then walked past them, not offering an explanation before he vanished down the path.

Neal's shoulder shook beneath her hand and Mary realized after a moment that it was a weak laugh. "No," Neal said wryly. "I'm sure it was just a regular spider."

CHAPTER 12

*N*eal knew he was a fool.

Graham may not hold the attack against him, but he'd humiliated himself in front of Mary and proved his unworthiness beyond a shadow of a doubt. He hadn't stopped to think when he saw the deer with Mary's clothing loose on its form. The flash of her fear had been driving his steps and, between his wolf snarling for freedom inside of him and the rush of adrenaline at the thought of his mate in danger, he'd made a snap attack, not pausing or assessing. It was the worst kind of behavior in a soldier—a terrible slip of control.

No one who was whole, who was thinking clearly, would have reacted so poorly. Surely Mary must know how broken he was now.

"I'm sorry."

Mary's hands on his shoulders felt like weights of guilt, like judgment, and Neal was surprised when she knelt in the damp grass beside him, one arm still draped around him.

The press of her body at his side was distracting. The

buttons of her blouse had popped off when she shifted and it hung loosely now, open in the front to show glimpses of her luscious breasts as she moved.

"You seem to apologize to me a lot," she observed without judgment.

"I'm broken," he said. The simple words came out without effort, and he was astonished by how much better he felt for having said them.

Mary didn't try to deny his words, and Neal was grateful for that. "Broken things are worth fixing," she said gently. "*You're* worth fixing. You don't have to be sorry, you just… have to let me in."

Neal lifted his eyes from the mesmerizing curves under her open blouse and looked into her face.

She looked back without wavering, which was something Neal couldn't do with his own reflection, and the compassion and emotion in her eyes undid something old and rusty in his chest.

"I don't know how to do that," he confessed. He could be nothing but truthful with her.

"Just trust me," Mary told him simply, as if trusting her was just that easy.

And unexpectedly, it was.

Morning flowed into noon as he told her everything— everything that had happened to him, and its consequences. It streamed from him in a rush of words that he couldn't stop and didn't try.

He told her everything backwards, from the escape of Beehag's prison to the terrible ten years of his stay there. The dart at his throat, and the journey to the Costa Rican island where he was caged and tormented into remaining in wolf form. He recounted the day he was in Columbia, on the first day of their mission to stop the turncoat Marine who was using school children to shelter his drug business. He even told her about Afghanistan, from years earlier, and the nightmares he had suffered ever since, and they laughed together about playing kick the can in the cul-de-sac, growing up in different small towns.

Mary added her own observations occasionally, but mostly she listened. Not once did she act shocked or judgmental about his revelations to her. She just absorbed everything he told her with solemn attention.

Neal's voice was raw and hoarse by the time he came to what he felt was the end of his narration, or the beginning. The sun, dappled through the plumeria tree above him, had burned off the clouds and dried the lawn. Downhill from them, the gazelle was grazing. She was in earshot, he thought, with those big dish-like ears, but strangely, the idea didn't bother him.

He sat with Mary in silence for a long moment. It felt comfortable and natural, as nothing had felt in a very long time. He'd gotten used to feeling tightly coiled and filled with anger, and he felt strangely empty now. Empty—and yet filled at the same time, because of the woman who sat beside him.

"You helped all the other shifters go home, after you were freed from the prison?" she finally asked.

"Almost all of them," Neal agreed, looking out over the green carpet to where the gazelle was pretending to ignore them.

"But not yourself."

Neal was silent, familiar tension rising in his throat.

"Does your old unit know what happened to you?'

"No."

Mary squeezed his arm. "They must think you went AWOL?"

"By now, they'd think I was dead," Neal guessed.

"You must be pretty angry about that."

Neal opened his mouth to deny it, then snapped it shut. He'd spent so much time trying not to think about it that he hadn't recognized how furious it all made him, or how much that frustration was leaking into all the other parts of his life.

Mary, with a thoughtful look that suggested she saw his revelation, went on. "I imagine you're pretty pissed that you never got revenge."

"Beehag died," Neal said shortly.

"His heart gave out over the antidote to a sedative. I don't imagine there was any satisfaction in that."

Neal realized his hands were balled in fists. He sighed and uncoiled them.

"Are you a therapist?" he asked, not entirely teasing. Some of the staff had tentatively suggested he talk to one, but they had stopped dropping hints after he reacted poorly.

"I'm a math teacher," Mary said with amusement. "At a middle school."

Neal saluted. "I should have known you worked in a combat zone."

"Because of the way I screamed about a spiderweb in my hair?" Mary's sideways look was rich with humor and self-deprecation.

Neal might have let her brush it off with humor, but their talk had left him raw and observant. She was genuinely embarrassed about her fear and felt bad for her reaction.

"I was the only deer shifter in a family of big cats, a throwback to a great-grandmother who was a deer," she explained shyly. "I guess I got used to being protected, and everyone … just expected me to be afraid of things. I think it's just a habit, now."

"It's okay to be afraid," he said roughly and, unexpectedly, it was true for more than just her.

Into the silence that fell after that, Mary's stomach rumbled audibly and she giggled. Neal let out a rusty guffaw with her, startling himself, and said, "It must be after lunch. Damn, I was supposed to help Travis with some cement work…"

They unwound themselves from each other and stood.

"You have to take care of yourself first," Mary said.

"Why do I get the feeling that's advice you don't always take?" Neal asked suspiciously.

He knew he was right by Mary's blush.

"I'll meet you later?" she deflected.

"I'll be working until late," Neal said apologetically.

"Then I'll meet you late."

"By the pool? I'll be closing the bar."

Mary nodded. "I'll be there."

An awkward moment of silence followed. Neal felt as if all the words had been dredged out of him and he had none left to offer.

"Later, then," Mary said shyly, and she moved to leave.

Neal couldn't let her leave like that and caught her after only a few steps for a passionate kiss. The blouse that had been barely staying together slipped off one shoulder at last. Her mouth was hungry under his, salty and tantalizing. Neal kissed her mouth and down her neck to that deliciously tempting bare shoulder, then went back to her lips for one final kiss before setting her back from him firmly.

"Later, then," he agreed, and he walked away with a rare smile at his mouth.

That was a proper goodbye.

CHAPTER 13

*M*ary got to the bar just before last call.

There were only a few guests left—a determinedly drunk elderly man with a thick Russian accent, and a cold blonde in high heels and little else. They both took Neal's last call as gospel and grumbled back to their cottages after downing unusual choices (he had something with an umbrella, and she had a vodka, straight). Spanish music played quietly from a tinny stereo behind the bar.

Mary took a shy seat at the counter.

"I just have to wash up a few glasses and wipe down the tables," Neal said.

"It's no problem," Mary said. It occurred to her that for the first time, his explanation had sounded more like a statement than an apology. She smiled, and the memory of his goodbye kiss made her squirm on her stool.

It was certainly no hardship watching him clear up. He scrubbed the tables with more vigor than skill, and the resort issue khaki shorts and polo shirt did nothing to hide the incredible physique beneath. Mary caught herself staring at his ass as he bent over to scrub a stubborn spot and had to look away before he turned back, blushing like a schoolgirl.

He toweled off the last clean glasses and put them away before he turned off the radio and flipped off the bar lights, plunging them into relative darkness.

Mary gave a little squeak of fear. "It's dark," she said, as he came around the bar to her. In the darkness, he was a little frightening, big and looming and featureless.

"I'll protect you," he offered, and his voice reassured her.

"I'd like that," Mary breathed.

Then he was gathering her into his arms for a kiss in greeting, and it was every bit as breathtaking as his goodbye kiss had been.

"It's starting to rain," she said, when she could again. Her eyes were starting to adjust to the darkness.

"Are you made of sugar?" Neal teased her.

Mary laughed. "No, but I am a little cold!"

"The pool is warm," Neal suggested.

"I didn't wear my swimsuit!" Mary protested.

"The resort *is* clothing optional," Neal pointed out. "Besides, I'm sure your underwear is less revealing than most of the bikinis I've seen here."

Mary sputtered. "Oh, I couldn't... it's... I could never..."

"Never say never," Neal persuaded.

Mary found herself drawn to the steps into the pool, flanked by the waterfalls. Running water and insects were the only sound outside of her own heartbeat that she could hear; the resort was otherwise quiet and anyone sensible was tucked into their beds, safe from the drizzling rain.

She let Neal pull off her shirt, enjoying the sharp intake he gave at the sight of her lacy bra, holding her breasts snugly. She shimmied out of her own shorts while Neal shed his own clothing down to briefs that did nothing to hide the impressive bulge of his cock.

"Sure you want me to stop?" he asked, putting a finger into his waistband teasingly.

Mary was quite sure she didn't, but she wasn't ready to admit that. "This is a terrible idea," she said, giggling like a misbehaving child. They crept down the grand steps to the water, and Neal pulled her down into the pool before she could balk.

Compared to the chilly night air and cool rain, the pool was warm and welcoming, and it glowed with blue orbs of lights underneath the surface. The effect as a whole was eerie and alien, and Mary felt deliciously not herself. Neal's hand was firm in her own and, when he tugged her closer, she glided to him willingly.

Her legs tangled around him and she pulled him close to kiss, unwittingly nearly dragging them under as they forgot about treading water in the passion of the moment.

They swam together for the edge of the pool near the waterfall where it grew shallower. Neal hooked an elbow on the ledge there and drew her close. They were protected from the view of anyone who might chance by on the bar deck, as slim a possibility as that was at this hour.

The sensation of the water all around her, her legs entwined with his, and the delicious pressure of his member against her nether areas was intoxicating. When Neal added his mouth, Mary found herself writhing in need.

"Don't stop," she begged him, when he pulled away, but then he touched her thighs with his hand, stroking at the edge of her lace panties and she could only whimper in pleasure.

She clung to his shoulders, panting and clawing at him as he used his talented hand to explore her through the wet fabric. When he finally slipped a questing finger under the elastic and into her folds, she gasped and cried out in release.

"If we weren't in the pool, you'd be able to tell how wet I am for you," she said near his ear when she could breathe again.

"Can you tell how hard I am for you?" he answered, and Mary found his proof with her own hand. He wasn't bulging now as much as he was straining against the soaked undergarment, his erect cock pulling the elastic away from his legs. There was little resistance from the underwear when Mary pushed it aside, the better to touch the firm, velvety flesh.

Floating in water was significantly different than tussling on the bed, and it meant a great deal more accidental touching as they struggled to keep their heads out of the water and their bodies in contact. Every touch was electric and new, caressed by the flow of water around them.

When Neal pulled aside her underwear and slipped into her, it was like being lit on fire. Even the friction of his member inside of her was new for being underwater, and the grip his hands felt fluid and different.

With touches and thrusts, he brought her to the crest of pleasure, not once, but twice, then pulled away, gasping, "Too hard…"

"Just hard enough," Mary laughed back at him, but she followed willingly to the far edge of the pool, and they tumbled out of the water onto the edge of the pool, where they kissed and touched and slipped on the wet tile. The rain had faded to nearly nothing.

Neal tugged her up onto one of the padded lounge

chairs, and Mary shimmied out of her underwear to welcome him, not sure where his briefs had disappeared to in the darkness, but glad they were gone. He slid fingers under her wet bra strap, and she gleefully unclipped it to let her breasts swing freely.

He worshipped them with his hands, cupping them and running thumbs over the erect nipples, and Mary felt her yearning reach another fever pitch.

He entered her in a rush, and Mary rose to greet him, moaning softly in satisfaction. Having him close, having him inside her, seemed to fulfill her in a way she'd never known she was missing.

Clever fingers and the perfect rhythm of thrusts brought her to peaks of pleasure again, and this time, Neal joined her at that crest of orgasm, and finally sank down to embrace her tenderly as their breath returned to normal.

CHAPTER 14

When the chill in the night air finally drove them off the damp lounge, Neal discovered that his briefs had been left behind in the pool and were floating just beyond the reach of the pool net.

After grumbling, Neal finally slipped back into the water and swam to retrieve them. Mary greeted him with a thick towel at the edge of the pool.

They walked the steps back up to the bar deck where they had shed their clothing and pulled them on. Neal couldn't help but stare while Mary dressed; all of her curves in the dim light were enchanting and mesmerizing while she struggled to get tight clothing over damp limbs.

He walked her to her cottage, hand-in-hand, running the last few steps as the rain started up again.

"Stay with me?" she asked softly as they stood in the doorway, almost begging.

Neal almost broke at the gentleness of her voice, feeling his heart aching inside him. He took her face in his hands for a gentle goodbye kiss.

"I... don't sleep restfully," he said regretfully.

"So I'll sleep in after you leave in the morning," Mary cajoled. "It's a big bed…"

Neal cut her off with a second kiss and a shake of his head. "Soon," he suggested, and he didn't want to think about how true that had to be given the little time they had left.

She didn't try again to persuade him, only gave him a curvy embrace and reluctantly let him go.

He left her sighing in the open door, lit from behind as he went back out into the dark, back to his own bunk to catch a few hours of sleep before waking to do the morning chores.

As promised, it was not restful sleep. He lay awake for far too long, thinking about how short his remaining time with Mary at the resort was. Her stay was only a few days more, and he…

While he couldn't imagine staying after she left, he also couldn't imagine fitting into her life. She was a math teacher. He was a broken soldier. She suited a quiet, domestic life. He wasn't fit for anything.

Close to dawn, he finally dozed off, and the afternoon's confessions dredged up terrible memories to work into nightmares of horror and guilt. He woke in a sweaty tangle of blankets, his pillow already ejected to the other side of the room.

He took a utilitarian shower in the tiny hotel bathroom, and when he went to pull on his clothing, he found the paper that Scarlet had given him in his pocket.

It was already worn; he must have taken it out and refolded it a dozen times over the past several days. Some of the pencil had rubbed off, but Neal had already committed the numbers to memory.

He could hear some of the other staff rising and heading off to work as he made his way to the empty common room. He could smell the breakfast that Chef must have been working on for several hours already.

The rain had let up, but it was still cool, and a thick mist lay over the resort. Neal tried to absorb some of the peacefulness from it as he lifted the receiver. While it rang through the international lines, Neal stared at the black TV screen across the room. Travis and Bastian had tried playing a shooter game with him a few weeks back, but his hands had shaken too much to aim at the animated bad guys. It was a far cry from his steady-handed sniper days.

When his unit commander, Judy Washburn, answered, her voice was a jarring reminder of his long-ago life.

For a moment, he could only consider that she probably wasn't still a major, and it seemed terribly important that he didn't know what rank she had now. He stabbed the button to hang up without speaking and buried his face in his hands.

He wasn't ready for this yet.

Mary would tell him he didn't have to be, he thought, and just the idea of her brought him back into balance. He could almost hear her voice in his ear, reminding him to take whatever time he needed. He didn't have to heal in a day.

He almost dialed again, but was interrupted by Travis, who walked briskly into the room and said, "Oh, good timing. I'll be needing your help at Cottage twelve this morning to get the new interior walls raised."

Travis said nothing about the phone that Neal still held in his hands, and Neal didn't volunteer anything.

"I'll be right there," Neal said, hanging up the receiver and standing.

"Neal."

They both turned to find Scarlet in the doorway. She

looked out of place in the shabby room, with the pearls at her throat and her starched linen skirt.

Neal stood at attention out of instinct and caught Travis doing the same out of a corner of his eye, though he didn't think that Travis had any military background.

"I'll need you out of the resort this afternoon." While Neal was still trying to process the speed of his ejection, Scarlet continued, "Go with Bastian on a mainland boat trip, or head out to clear the waterfall trail, I don't care, but don't come back until late tonight or even tomorrow."

Neal furrowed his eyebrows. If he wasn't being thrown out…

"I've got an investor coming here with Beehag's heir, Benedict, and I don't want any… *incidents*."

"I don't know what you think I would…"

Scarlet raised a silencing hand. "This is not a topic that is open for discussion."

Neal remembered Mary's quiet assessment that he'd never gotten revenge and surprised them all with a grim smile. "Yes, Ma'am."

Scarlet nodded and swept out as abruptly as she'd come.

"We'd better get to work while we can then," Travis said, looking bemused.

"Right you are," Neal said cheerfully.

CHAPTER 15

*M*ary couldn't swim her laps without blushing and remembering the night before in vivid detail, so it wasn't long before she was crawling out of the water and toweling off more vigorously than usual. Neal had been nowhere to be found since breakfast, but the head waiter had winked at her and said, "He'll find you for lunch."

Scarlet-cheeked, Mary slipped her sundress on over her damp suit and went to the bar for a cold water.

Tex was behind the bar, strumming melancholy chords on his guitar along with the radio, but he put it down as she approached.

"What can I get you, darlin'?" he drawled.

"Just ice water, please," Mary said, putting the towel carefully over the barstool before she sat.

"Coming right up." Tex reached up to get the glass and filled it with a swift scoop of glittering ice from the ice bin.

Mary wondered how much he knew, or if anyone had caught sight—or sound—of their pool activities the night before.

"We're all happy to see Neal smiling again," Tex said warmly as he put the sweating glass down in front of her.

Mary's cheeks felt even hotter. "I, uh. Yes, me too. I mean, it's a great smile."

"I wouldn't flirt with that bartender." Neal's voice surprised her from behind, and Mary swiveled on her stool to find him standing at the back entrance, shirtless and dirty and sweaty.

It was a heady combination, and Mary wondered exactly how red her face could become.

She gulped down some of her cold water as Tex protested, "Come on, now. Why shouldn't she flirt with me?"

"You're unlucky in love," Neal reminded him.

"It's a tragic truth," Tex agreed mournfully. "You're better off with this one," he said to Mary.

"I think so, too," Mary squeaked.

Neal's shirtless proximity was terribly distracting.

"I thought we might take the boat out snorkeling this afternoon," Neal told her, accepting his own glass of water from Tex and downing it in a few determined gulps.

Mary felt the color finally drain from her face. "Oh no," she protested. "I don't... not in the *ocean*. I couldn't."

Neal shrugged. "We could head over to the mainland with Travis, then. Do some shopping, or take the horseback shore tour."

"Horseback?" Mary shivered. "I can't ride. They're so big, and no. No. I can't. I don't need to go shopping. No. Boats, no. Can't."

Tex and Neal blinked at her.

"I'm afraid of boats," she confessed sheepishly, feeling their surprised scrutiny.

Tex found some glasses to wipe, politely looking away.

"It's perfectly safe," Neal suggested, looking baffled at her terror, but her look must have expressed her distrust adequately. He counter-offered, "How about a hike, then? There's an easy loop that goes up by a really gorgeous waterfall. It's about five miles, no boats. We'll take a picnic lunch."

Mary wanted to balk. There were bugs, and snakes, and scorpions out there in the wild jungle, and she'd already had closer relations with a spider than she ever wanted to again. But she didn't want Neal to think she was a complete ninny, either.

"That sounds nice," she said weakly.

"I'll grab a shower and get us a bagged lunch," Neal said briskly.

"I'll change clothes and pack a few things," Mary offered with a brave smile. How bad could it be?

'A few things' proved to be her entire purse stuffed full, and Mary was glad she had opted for the kind that swung over a shoulder; bottles of water were heavy and she wasn't planning to go out without sunscreen and bug spray, or the pocket first aid kit. Spare socks and her raincoat made the bag bulky and awkward. When Neal caught sight of her, his expression said more than he needed to.

He was carrying a single water bottle in one of the cargo pockets of his shorts and, aside from the wicked-looking machete that hung from his belt and the promised lunch, appeared to have nothing else extra on him.

Mary had changed into long, lightweight travel pants and sneakers. She wished she'd brought heavier shoes, especially once they had hiked out the first mile.

Neal's idea of an easy walk was clearly not her own, even though they stopped several times for Neal to hack back the encroaching jungle vines.

Mary was sweating and itchy and hating the smell of the bug spray she had saturated herself with by the time they stopped for lunch. She picked a rock to sit on that at least gave her a view of any insects that might try to sneak up on her and could barely eat the lunch that Neal had packed for keeping an eye on the beetles and ants that were crawling around on the jungle floor. The dappled light through the jungle canopy made everything look as if it were always moving, and Mary spent the meal trying not to twitch at every rustle and skittering leaf.

"I'm sorry," Neal told her, as they were finally packing up the dirty wrappers. The crumbs were swarmed by ants in a terrifying show of swift insect utility.

"There you go apologizing again," Mary said with a weak attempt at a laugh.

"You're not having fun."

"I'm not an outdoors person," Mary confessed. "I'm sorry."

Neal looked conflicted. "We could go back, but I'm supposed to stay away from the resort until Beehag's heir is off the property tonight."

Mary forgot the bugs momentarily, staring at him in shock. She recalled their conversation from earlier, when she'd pointed out he'd never had his revenge for what Beehag had done to him. "Oh. I can see why Scarlet might not want you around for that."

Then it occurred to her. "We'll be out here until *tonight*? After *dark*?" She hadn't brought a flashlight and the idea of these big, looming trees after dark, and all the *things* that would be hiding among them, was enough to bring her to hysterics.

"I plan to be back right about sunset," Neal said soothingly.

"Oh," Mary hiccuped. "Okay."

She lifted her chin. "I can do that."

It didn't sound as bold as she would have liked it to, but Neal smiled at her in a way that melted her knees, and she felt able to sling her bag across her body and start hiking again.

CHAPTER 16

$\mathcal{N}$ eal watched Mary trudge courageously in front of him, distracted by the sway of her hips and the glimpses he got of the curve of her ass. He wished she had brought less with her, mostly because the bulky bag covered his view.

He wanted to praise her bravery, for continuing to hike out in a wilderness she was clearly terrified of, but he was fairly sure she wouldn't believe him, and he didn't want it to sound like empty flattery.

Shortly after their lunch, it began to rain. At first it was a light drizzle that they heard on the leaves above them more than they felt, but within fifteen minutes, it had turned into a deluge. Mary put on her raincoat.

"I'm glad I brought this after all," she said cheerfully, pulling the hood over her head. "I know you thought I brought too much."

Neal was wise enough not to agree with her.

It was still warm, so Neal didn't mind that he was shortly soaking wet, but it slowed their progress as the ground became slick and hazardous.

The trail itself was not wide, knobby roots were constant obstacles to clamber over, and the moss grew slippery as the rain continued.

Conversation proved difficult, between their concentration on walking and the noise of the rain; the jungle canopy acted like percussion under the raindrops, and the fall of the rain was all collected on leaves that would then dump on them unceremoniously when full of water.

Mary struggled on gamely and offered Neal an overly-bright smile whenever their glances crossed.

This was a terrible idea, he told himself. *Way to go, Romeo.*

He would have berated himself further, but then they rounded the corner of the trail and there was an opening in the trees. The view suddenly expanded, showing a tiny cove below, cradled by cliffs, and the waterfall he'd wanted to show her when he'd suggested the hike. Everything was shrouded in mist, so the ocean below was reduced to a single line of breakers before vanishing and the sky above melted into foggy trees above them.

The waterfall itself was a silver ribbon from the cliff to their right, crashing past them down to the sliver of beach below.

"Oh!" Mary said beside him. Her fingers found his as they stared. "It was worth it."

If he had not been standing right beside her, Neal would not have heard her over the fierce roar of the little fall and the pounding of the ocean.

He looked at her skeptically. "Are you sure?"

Her hair, once neatly braided, was wild and half-loose, plastered against her wet face. Neal wasn't sure what was sweat and what was rain. Even her raincoat was limp in the wet, and her pants clung to her curves. But her face, already red-cheeked, had lit up at the gorgeous view, and

Neal thought that she looked utterly gorgeous in all her disarray.

"I'm sure," she said, giving Neal an impulsive hug, a little hindered by her soggy purse and wet raincoat.

He squeezed her tightly in return, and the curves of her body pressed against him made him forget the miserable trip and even the beautiful view. When she might have drawn away, he kissed her, and she wrapped her arms more tightly around his neck and kissed him in return.

Her mouth tasted like honey and promises, and her breasts beneath the crinkly raincoat were firm against his chest. Neal was tempted to peel her out of it right then and there and lay her down on the jungle floor to make love to her on the spot. He settled for caressing her through the unwieldy garment.

"It was definitely worth it," Mary declared with a smile, once he had released her.

"We do still have to walk back," Neal cautioned. The rain had reduced to a faint drizzle again, and he even thought it might be clearing in one area of the foggy sky above them.

Mary winced. "The same way?"

Neal shook his head, and showed Mary where the trail switched back behind them. "It's a little steep down here, and then we'll be walking back along the cliffs to the resort."

Mary looked dubious. "Along… the cliffs? Are they very high?"

Neal noticed that she was staying well away from the drop off by the waterfall. He wouldn't be surprised if she were afraid of heights, too. "Oh, no," he reassured her. "Twenty-five feet or so above the ocean?" They were twice that high here.

"That doesn't sound so bad," she squeaked, and she

turned to lead the way down the steep switchback. One side of the trail was tight against the path they'd just followed and the other dropped away over the little cove. It was narrow, narrower than the last time Neal remembered walking here, and rainwater runoff was spilling down from the upper path. The earth was soft and spongy underfoot, beneath the slick surface.

It took Neal a moment to put all the warning signs together, and just as he opened his mouth to caution Mary, the trail beneath her crumbled away into nothing.

Moving as only a shifter could, Neal reached for her and pulled her back to solid ground—only to find that the ground he'd assumed solid was anything but, and then they were both falling, crashing and sliding down the side of the cliff to the jungle foliage below.

Neal, still holding onto Mary's arm, rolled to protect her. It was a far cry from his experiences of jumping from aircraft, hindered by Mary and her handbag and distinctly missing a parachute, but he was able to turn them so that she was protected in his arms, just as they crashed into the first of the trees.

Branches whipped them across every exposed surface and snapped beneath them, jarring impact after jarring impact that Neal could only grit his teeth and weather. One against his head had him seeing stars, then another smashed against an elbow, but all he could think was that he had to keep Mary safe, at any cost.

Air was impossible to draw into lungs. Every blow drove it out again. Then there was blazing pain and he lost his brief battle with consciousness.

CHAPTER 17

*M*ary left her eyes shut even after they'd at last been lying still for a long moment, catching her breath and trying to make sense of the last few crazy moments. Neal had only let her go at the very last moment, and they lay close enough together that she could hear his labored breathing.

When she finally opened her eyes, she was alarmed by how pale and still he looked as he lay in the sand and the awkward angle of his body. She moved to sit up, and cried out in surprised pain. The arm of her raincoat was ripped open and a broad gash beneath was oozing blood. Her shoulder felt wrenched and, when she tested the rest of her limbs, she suspected a sprained ankle—if it wasn't actually broken. Her sides ached and she guessed she would be peppered in bruises the following day.

She glanced up at the tree they had fallen through, littered with fresh broken branches, and the cliff beyond. Shrouded in fog, it looked very high above them indeed. The scar of the mudslide they had started was darker than the rest of the rock around it.

It was a miracle that they had survived.

Neal groaned, and Mary scooted to his side just as his eyes fluttered open.

"Are you okay?" she asked, feeling ridiculous the second the words were out of her mouth.

"Are *you*… okay?" he asked in response, voice rough and weak.

"I'm fine," she said, and she had to laugh a little in relief that he could speak. At no other time in her life would she have considered her current state 'fine.'

She winced to see that all of his exposed skin had been whipped raw by the tree. Several of them qualified as gashes, bleeding freely. He lay oddly, still looking dazed, and Mary struggled to remember her first aid training.

"I'm going to look you over," she said properly.

Neal started to try to sit up. Mary told him sharply, "No! Let me have a look first!"

He protested less than Mary thought he should, sinking back into the sand with a low sound of pain.

Starting at his head, she found the lump at the base of his neck that was probably the cause of his dazed state. He moaned when she touched his chest and offered, "Probably a broken rib."

She was gentle, working her fingers down his side, but he still sucked his breath in sharply and added, "Maybe two."

Moving his elbow made him give a hiss of pain as she examined his arms. Mary suspected a sprain. At any other time, she would have been delighted for the excuse to run her fingers over the magnificent muscles, but now, she was simply concerned for him. None of the abrasions seemed major, and she moved to his chest and stomach, not finding any problems. His legs lay in odd ways, but he was able to help her move them straight, which is when Mary found the worst of his problems.

"Oh," she said in quiet alarm.

"Hurts," Neal admitted shortly.

"You… landed on your machete," Mary said, moving the tool out of the way. Blood was flowing down into the sand below him. The wound was along the outside of his right hip. She didn't think he could have nicked the artery, but the amount of blood was alarming. "I don't know how bad it is, but Neal, you should shift."

"*Don't ever tell me to do that!*"

Mary rocked back on her ankles, not even minding the shooting pain as she did so. Neal was snarling, pulling away from her. "No, don't move!" she said, alarmed at how the bleeding ramped up as he struggled.

His eyes were feral and filled with pain, but Mary could not let him drive her away. "You lie still," she said, as firmly and gently as she could. "I'll do what I can."

Neal subsided, the wildness in his eyes fading to only agony, and Mary unclipped the machete from his belt to use it to cut away the rest of his shorts.

The injury was shallow, she was glad to find, but it was dirty and bleeding merrily, even as his other scrapes and wounds seemed to be slowing. She balanced the machete between her knees and was able to cut her shirt—the only passingly dry article of clothing between them—into a bandage, but it wouldn't be long enough to tie around his massive leg. She could tie the arms of her raincoat around him. It had stopped raining, at least.

She knew she ought to clean the wound first. "I'm going to get water," she said.

Neal only growled.

Her handbag had been thrown clear, and Mary limped

over and dumped it unceremoniously onto the sand to find her water bottles. One was empty, but the other was nearly full. It would have to be enough—she didn't trust the water from the waterfall, and she knew that seawater wouldn't do. She scooped up the first aid kit, too, wishing she'd brought a larger one.

Neal made a guttural noise as she washed out the wound. She wasn't satisfied with the way the sparse water washed out the ugly flap of skin, but short of other choices, Mary didn't know what else to do. The little drizzle of water seemed to get out most of the grit, and Mary squeezed the two tiny packets of antibiotic onto the gash. It looked like pathetically little against the long slice.

She folded her shirt onto the wound and wrapped the raincoat around it, tying the arms as tight as they would go.

She stepped back. "Well, that's hideous," she said. "But hopefully it will do."

Neal gave an attempt at a laugh, but it turned into a dry cough and he lapsed into pained silence.

Mary completed her examination down his legs to his feet, but found nothing else of great concern.

She returned to his head, frowning. "Neal, I'm going to shift."

"Fine," he said shortly. "Just don't ever ask me to."

"You'll heal much…"

"*Don't*. Ever."

Mary knew a losing argument when she was in one, and backed away. She took off her soggy shoes and socks, wincing as her ankle protested the activity. Her own aches and pains were back with a vengeance and even the simple act of undressing was agony.

She looked up to catch Neal watching her with warm eyes.

"You're beautiful," he said in a whisper.

Mary blushed. "Oh, no. I know I'm not." She wanted to cover herself, but something about the reverence in Neal's eyes as he looked at her made her hesitate to do so, instead letting Neal watch as she unclipped her bra and tried to get out of her soaked pants and underwear without angering any of her worst injuries.

"How could you think that?" Neal asked her.

Mary was so surprised by the question that she answered it frankly. "Well, I'm fat." She had to sit down to pull the legs of her pants off, her ankle too fragile to support all her weight at such an awkward angle.

He laughed at her, and it was the most encouraging sound she'd heard from him since their fall. "You are not fat, you are glorious, and I adore every curve," he protested. "*Magnolia* is fat, and she is the second most beautiful woman at Shifting Sands, so your argument has no meaning at all."

Mary had no counter for that. She couldn't doubt his sincerity and it pleased her more than she thought it ought to please a modern, independent woman. "My hair is limp," she added, but it sounded as ridiculous to her ears as it did to Neal's—she knew it was plastered to her face with rain and sweat, and she could tell by the stinging of her face when she smiled that it was as whipped with branches as Neal's was. She gave a mock falsetto and continued merrily, "My makeup is simply ruined, and my dress! Oh, my stars, I could never go to the ball like this!"

Neal chuckled, as he was supposed to, and sobered as his ribs reminded him how much that hurt.

"Seriously though," Mary said, "I am going to shift now and wander around to see about how we're going to get out of here."

"You do," Neal said shortly, clearly in pain.

Mary hesitated. She had never shifted in front of anyone but family before and she felt terribly self-conscious.

Then she was thinking about grazing and leaping and sun on her flanks, and was walking forward as a deer.

CHAPTER 18

*M*ary as a deer was a beautiful as she was as a human. Her brown coat was smooth and glossy, and her big ears were expressive and mobile.

She came over and touched Neal with her whiskered muzzle, then pranced away, limping only slightly.

Neal was glad when she disappeared through the brush towards the base of the waterfall, because he knew he'd done a dismal job of holding himself together in front of her, and he didn't want to admit just how much agony he was in. The leg that had been cut was like a throbbing fire, but the pain in his chest worried him much more.

Every breath caused a stabbing pain, and there was a tightness to his chest and dizziness that Neal strongly suspected was a collapsed lung—if not fully, at least partially. They had no sort of catheter to release the pressure he was feeling, so he saw no reason to admit it to Mary. Let her keep believing it was just a few broken ribs and a concussion. He couldn't bear to see her worry, and there was no treatment here that could fix an injury like that.

You could shift, his brain betrayed him. Deep inside, Neal could feel his red maned wolf stir.

Neal snarled and refused to think of it any further. He drew himself slowly into a sitting position, verifying with each dry cough and agonizing breath that his diagnosis was correct.

There was an old piece of driftwood that had been flung up high on the beach, and it had a root piece that was exactly the angle of a reclined easy chair. Neal managed to drag himself over to it and prop himself into the crook, just as the deer returned and shifted seamlessly into Mary.

"You shouldn't be moving!" she said in alarm.

Neal grunted. "Got tired of the view there. This one is better."

The sun was fighting through the clouds and fog, and blue sky was beginning to show above the mist. Late afternoon sunlight made the little cove glow. In truth, Neal would have been hard pressed to pick a more lovely scene. Golden-white sand in a perfect semi-circle met gentle ocean, lapping at its edges. Emerald jungle plants fringed the bottom of dark cliffs on all sides, and the waterfall they had hiked to see made a silver ribbon that fell down the cliff and crawled to the ocean like a bit of discarded Christmas wrapping on the sand.

"I'm beginning to reconsider what I said about the view being worth the hike," Mary said. "But it does seem to be doing its best to be picturesque."

She frowned at him and felt his forehead, and then carefully untied the raincoat. She didn't pull off the shirt bandage, but seemed satisfied that it hadn't soaked through with blood and re-tied the raincoat.

"I guess we'll want a fire," she suggested, leaning back on her ankles without wincing. She moved more easily now and the raw vine whips on her face had faded significantly, even more than Neal would have expected from a shifter's ability to self-heal. "And some food? I have two granola bars left."

"Water," Neal suggested, concentrating on not coughing. His lungs were crying for more air that he couldn't get, and it was making him dizzy.

"I can fill the bottles at the waterfall," Mary said dubiously. "I had a good drink as a deer, but we ought to boil it for you."

She said it without being pointed, but Neal still winced and set his teeth, ready for a fight about shifting again.

Mary stood up and walked to where she'd left her clothing. She held up the soggy garments, clearly decided not to put them back on, and spread them on the driftwood to dry instead. The fog was burning off quickly, and the heat of the sun was drying a halo of gold from the hair that had escaped her braid.

Watching her gather up the contents of her bag and sort them neatly for inventory was a treat when she was nude, and she seemed to lack self-consciousness about it for the first time.

"The wood is too wet to use friction to start a fire," Neal said. He didn't think it mattered if he drank contaminated water given state of the rest of him, but building a fire would give Mary something to do. "Do you have any lenses?"

"I have sunglasses," Mary suggested.

"No good, they have to be clear." Neal looked at the odd selection of things. "You brought condoms?"

Mary blushed. "I thought this was going to be a romantic hike, not a death march through the rain capped by falling down a cliff," she said tartly.

Neal laughed and gritted his teeth at the pain of it.

When the wave of dizziness had passed, he explained, "We can use that to start a fire."

Mary blinked at him. "A condom?"

"A condom full of water," Neal added.

"This is why I like math," Mary complained. "Math makes sense."

Neal smiled but didn't attempt another laugh. "I'll show you. We'll need dry tinder, and good kindling, and water."

Mary stood. "I can get those."

She scooped up the two empty bottles and the cavernous handbag. "There were some driftwood piles at the other end of the beach that might be dry in the middle. I'll try there first."

Neal lost his battle against the urge to cough and regretted it, able to do nothing but helplessly watch her walk away.

CHAPTER 19

*M*ary didn't like the Neal's pallor or the rattle of his dry cough, but she knew that was nothing she could treat.

The sand was getting warm beneath her bare feet, and wading through the cool stream was unexpectedly pleasant. Mary paused at the first pile of driftwood. There were probably things in the dark recesses of the wood—biting things and maybe even venomous things. She gritted her teeth, wished she was wearing her soaked clothes, and reached in to rattle a few branches loose, snatching her hand back quickly.

No swarms of snakes or spiders came pouring out at her and, after a moment, Mary tackled it again, pulling the wet wood off the top to reveal a dry inner cavern with an armload of good driftwood. She filled her bag, before adding some of the crunchy dry seaweed she found there, hopeful it would make good tinder. The second heap of driftwood was wet through, but there was an overhang at the end of the beach that had a pile of larger pieces. She heaped her arms full of them, and only as she was returning to the stream did she realize that she hadn't poked the pile or checked it for bugs before she picked it up.

Her skin crawled at the idea she might be carrying ants or spiders, and she dropped her armload unceremoniously by the stream. She filled both her water bottles and capped them, then gathered her wood back up more carefully, flicking a single tiny ant off with a leaf.

The fog had burned off by the time she returned to Neal with her treasures, and she was relieved to see that his driftwood prop was at least partially in the shade. He was dozing, though his face, even in sleep, was still twisted with pain.

Mary gathered up some rocks, only once biting back a shriek of terror when she disturbed the creature—she wasn't sure what it was—which was living beneath it.

Though she suspected it wasn't necessary, she built a fire ring with the rocks, and was pleased at how domestic and camp-like their little space looked with the addition.

Neal woke, and was appropriately pleased by her building efforts. He walked her through setting out the wood for the fire and pouring the condom partly full of water.

"You're essentially making a lens with it," he explained.

Mary made a tiny nest of the seaweed tinder and squeezed the pocket of water in the condom until she got two tiny points of light that she could focus together.

"Hold it just a few inches away," Neal advised. "Have you ever burnt ants with a magnifying glass?"

"No," Mary said with disgust. "I have definitely never done that."

Neal chuckled and then coughed, swearing under his

breath. Mary resisted the urge to drop her make-shift firestarter and go comfort him.

When his coughing subsided, there was still nothing happening. "How long does this take?"

"It could take a while," Neal said hoarsely. "A long while, I'm afraid. It's a game of patience now, and the sun is past its strongest point."

Mary settled into a more comfortable position. "Alrighty then."

There was a moment of silence, and Mary listened to the pound of the ocean on the shore and the noise of the waterfall and concentrated on holding her points of light still on the seaweed.

"Tell me about one of your missions," she finally suggested, not wanting to watch Neal lapse back into sleep. "How about that last one you were on?"

For a moment, she thought he was going to refuse, but then he started speaking, slowly and carefully. "The short version of the story is that we were stopping a drug lord in South America."

"That sounds exciting."

"The longer version, which I will spare you, involves an AWOL Marine, Lewis, who had set himself up as a local kingpin, a school being used as a switchhouse, and a mysterious billionaire funder."

"That version sounds even more exciting!"

Even with his breath shallow and his words unnaturally slow, Neal had a wonderful storytelling voice.

"Lewis knew we were coming, somehow, and he knew that some of us were shifters. He used children as hostages and made us surrender ourselves before we could call in for support."

Mary whistled. "That doesn't sound good."

"It wasn't. Major Washburn—Judy—was fitted with some new tech that we didn't want them getting their hands on, so we staged her suicide."

Mary gasped.

"It was a ruse, don't worry. Ended up luring in one of the mercenaries and blowing up half the compound. We focused on getting the kids out and were able to call for backup once we were on high ground."

"Did you get Lewis? Did everyone get away?"

"I don't know," Neal admitted with frustration in his hoarse voice. "I was darted in the neck during our escape. Lewis is the type to throw every man, or child, he has at his own escape, so it wouldn't surprise me if he was still on the loose."

Mary had no answer for that, guessing that he felt guilty for not being able to protect his teammates. She lapsed into silence, staring at the point of light focused on the seaweed.

It was several moments before she realized that it was starting to squirm, and she squealed so loudly that Neal startled.

"It's smoking! It's smoking! What do I do?"

It was everything she could manage not to drop the condom in her excitement.

"You'll want to blow on it, very gently, to encourage a flame, and immediately feed it the smallest kindling," Neal explained.

Mary leaned over awkwardly, holding the condom water balloon in one hand and tiny tinder in the other, giving it a cautious puff of air. Her heart fell as the smoke danced and seemed to disappear, then gave a whoop of triumph when the tiniest flicker of flame appeared.

It vanished almost immediately back into smoke, but a

second, more careful puff of air brought it back, and Mary fed it tiny dry twigs with trembling hands.

"It worked!" she crowed. In no time, she had a small, happily crackling fire, and Mary felt like she had just conquered a country or taken down her own drug lord.

CHAPTER 20

atching Mary's little triumphs was the best thing that Neal had ever witnessed. He'd been in survival situations more dire than this, but it meant a hundred times more to her to do something basic like make a fire than it ever had to him. Each task was a tangible victory, and Neal loved watching her face scrunch in concentration and light up in celebration.

Once she'd gotten the fire going, she put an empty mint tin and her sunglasses case to work as vessels for boiling water, using a sock for a potholder. They boiled quickly, and she set them aside to cool before putting them into the plastic bottle. She hummed as she worked, clearly proud of her accomplishments and delighted with every little success she managed.

If she couldn't quite mask her concern for him, Neal didn't blame her. His chest felt like it was wrapped in steel bands that were being tightened by the minute. Every breath was painful and difficult. He knew that if he hadn't been a shifter, he would already have been dead, and the possibility still existed that he wouldn't weather an injury of this gravity. He wasn't even sure if shifting would help him now, and he continued to refuse to think of it as an option.

"I thought we could split one of the granola bars tonight and save the other for tomorrow morning," Mary offered, bringing the foil-wrapped treat to Neal with her hard-won half-bottle of boiled water.

Neal wondered how much of his dizziness was hunger. He certainly didn't feel like he had much of an appetite, but it had been a long time since their picnic lunch. He drank the still-warm water gratefully and held out a hand for the offered food. Mary broke it in halves and gave him the larger chunk.

Neal didn't have the energy to argue with her or try to insist she take the larger portion, and he suspected she'd completely refuse it anyway. He chewed the sugary bar obediently.

"Do you think they've noticed we're gone yet? They'll probably start looking for us first thing in the morning, don't you think?" Mary suggested, sitting beside him carefully.

The sun was just beginning to go down, casting long shadows along the beach towards them.

"Yes," Neal said soothingly. "At dawn, no doubt."

He didn't consider the worrisome idea that Travis had taken the boat to the mainland for an overnight, and that Scarlet probably thought they were on it and not due back until tomorrow afternoon. Only Tex knew that he'd changed his plans to take a hike instead. When would Tex notice that they were missing? It was hard to think past the pounding pain in his head and the vertigo that was swamping him.

"It'll be dark soon," Mary said. Neal could hear the quail in her voice before she steeled it to add, "I want to take another look at your leg, while there's still enough light."

Neal let her unwrap it and peel off the shirt.

"I think it looks better," she said uncertainly, poking gently. "A little, anyway." Blood still oozed along it, but it was sluggish compared to the original flow and the shirt wasn't completely soaked. It didn't look infected, at least. "Let's put the clean socks on for bandages now, and I'll wash this blouse out so we can use it tomorrow if we need it."

She stood, brushing sand off of her legs briskly. She put on her pants and bra, now that they were dry; the sun was losing its strength as it plunged for the horizon, and she put most of the remaining wood onto the fire. "I'll get another load of wood and water, too."

"Mary," Neal said, as she started to stride away. "I'm proud of you."

She was back at his side in a flash. "Don't talk like that," she said fiercely.

Neal was trying to fight back one of the wracking coughs that his battered lungs were insisting they needed. "Like what?"

"Like you don't expect to be here when I get back." There were tears in her blue eyes, gathered but unfallen. "I'm not blind. I know you're more hurt than you'll admit. I know I can't help you, and you won't help yourself, but damn it! Neal, you'd better hold on until someone else can get here and help you, because I'm not willing to lose you."

Neal felt like the band on his chest tightened three notches, and he envied Mary her easy sobs. "I'll fight to the last," he promised. "I'm too tough to die here."

"I'll hold you to that," she said fiercely, clinging to one hand and bending over him. "I didn't chase you across half the resort just to let you get away this easily."

Neal wheezed a laugh for her. "I've never been so happy to be caught."

Mary sniffed and drew in a deep breath before standing. "It's almost dark. I have to get wood while I can." Neal wasn't sure if the tremor in her voice was fear or some other emotion, but he marveled at the way she squared her shoulders and marched off into the growing gloom.

CHAPTER 21

*T*he cheerful afternoon sun was gone, and the final direct rays had vanished by the time Mary made it to the stream. She refilled her water bottles and tucked them to the bottom of her voluminous bag. The stream was less friendly in the dark—no longer a Christmas trimming, but a stream of blood, reflecting the final light of the sunset. She rolled up her pants to wade across it cautiously.

The last light was gone by the time she made it across, and it took her eyes several moments to adjust. Every shadow seemed full of chirping insects and singing frogs, and every bush rustled with some sort of creature in it. Continuing to walk forward was one of the hardest things she had ever done. Behind her was Neal and the safe, cheerful glow of her fire, but before her was darkness and mystery and danger.

There was a bright moon overhead, so she wasn't walking entirely in blackness, but the shadows were thick. Mary wanted to walk further away from the treeline than she had in the daylight, and was alarmed to discover that the tide had come in: the beach was a much thinner sliver than it had been earlier, and the terrifying ocean was threatening to encroach on the places she wanted to walk.

A tiny crab skittered across her path, making Mary startle and bite back a shriek. The last thing she needed was to make Neal try to come after her.

The thought steadied her.

Neal needed her.

She had to be brave for Neal.

She marched forward again, and faced down the menacing driftwood piles with a determined scowl. "I don't like you, and you don't like me," she told them fiercely. "But I need wood, and I teach middle school, so nothing you can do can scare me off."

As declarations of bravery went, it lacked panache, but the ridiculousness of it buoyed her spirits and Mary was able to plunge her arms into the unknown depths and find more wood that was dry to the touch. The sun had even dried some of the driftwood she had rejected earlier.

She couldn't see each piece well enough to identify bugs, so she could only brush at each one and try not to image that each little tickle was something with too many legs and antenna.

She filled her bag to bursting and piled more into her arms before turning back towards their piece of the beach —and stopped in alarm.

The tide had come in even further as she worked, and where there had once been a clear path back to their fire, there was now ocean, lapping right up to the trees in places.

She could try to scramble back into dense jungle foliage, or she could wade through dark water—dark *ocean* water. Dark ocean water that was probably teeming with biting, stinging things.

Mary took a tighter grip on her armload of wood. Trying to climb through the jungle— which was undoubtedly full of scorpions and snakes—would be nearly impossible with her load of firewood.

She stopped to roll her pants up further, up above her knees, and as she was patting them smooth, recognized that she was just trying to delay the inevitable.

"I teach middle school," she reminded herself.

She gathered up all of her wood again and settled her bag firmly across her body.

Then she stepped into the lapping water and waded across to the other side of the crescent.

Walking in the ocean was not like wading in a stream. The stream knew where it wanted to go and went merrily there. But the ocean was a different matter altogether.

The ocean caressed her. It tickled at her, and swirled around her ankles, and tried to take the sand away from the bottoms of her toes. It surged up almost to her knees and tried to pull her out with it in a salty partners dance. It subsided and relented and teased her, making her shiver as it played against her bare skin. Mary closed her eyes, willing herself just to keep going—and then she was walking out of it, close to Neal's driftwood chair, and she could see the glow of her fire on the undersides of the trees again. Licking her lips, Mary wondered now why she had been so frightened. The ocean against her legs hadn't harmed her. In fact, it had felt… almost nice.

She actually stopped and turned around, dipping her toes into the lacy foam right at the edge. It was partly greeting and partly in thanks. She knew she would never have to fear the ocean again.

CHAPTER 22

*T*rue to his promise, Neal was still conscious when Mary returned with her heaped armload of driftwood, but it was more of a fight than he liked to admit.

She dropped her burden beside the fire, shimmying out from her laden bag strap in a manner that would have boiled Neal's blood if he were in better shape. She was lit by the cheerfully crackling fire in warm hues that accentuated every gorgeous curve, and there was moonlight giving her a cool halo from behind. Clad only in torn pants and a bra, she was all womanly perfection in shape and grace. Even half-dead, he wanted her to the very core of his being.

"How are you feeling?" she asked, kneeling beside him.

"I've been better," Neal said truthfully. "But I'm not worse."

If he kept his breaths painfully shallow, he could keep the chest-buckle feeling from reaching excruciating levels, and the worst of the coughs seem to have passed. Maybe he was just getting used to fighting them back.

Mary felt his forehead and Neal willed himself to think cooling thoughts. He could feel her frown through the darkness.

"Neal," she started.

"I'm not shifting," he growled at her. At this point, he wasn't even sure if he could; it had been so long since he'd had a hint of his inner wolf that he wasn't sure any of it was left. Could a shifter lose his animal self?

"I won't ask," Mary said. "But …"

Neal gave a growl, sure that the 'but' would involve shifting.

"Remember your promise," Mary said simply. "Just keep fighting. I love you, and I don't want to lose you."

Neal lost a precious breath at her words and had to cough again. Mary held his shoulders while he struggled back to his precarious balance of shallow breathing, dizzy to the bottom of his soul.

She loved him.

Neal knew he ought to say it back, that he ought to confess that the tangled up mess of his heart was all hers, whether she understood everything that entailed or not, but he couldn't.

She was everything to him already, but when he thought about telling her that, it felt like he was ensnaring her, trapping her in the miserable downward spiral of his life. He couldn't tell her. He could barely admit it to himself.

He closed his eyes when Mary went to put more wood on the fire, missing her presence beside him as soon as she was gone.

Nothing used to scare him. He took the most dangerous jobs without quailing, faced the most terrible enemies. Now here he was, facing mortality with the woman he was afraid to love, and he was more terrified of admitting to himself that he cared about her than he was of the cold reality of his death drawing near.

He felt Mary return, warm against his side. She shivered and then shifted, laying her gentle deer's head on his good thigh.

I love you, he thought he heard, like a distant echo, or a memory.

CHAPTER 23

*M*ary woke in darkness.

The moon was gone, and the sprinkle of stars in the bottomless sky did little but frost the edges of the shadows.

For a terrible moment, she thought that Neal's stillness beneath her head was complete, and she shifted to her human form as she sat up.

He was still breathing, but if his breaths had been shallow before, they were almost nothing now. His skin felt clammy and chilled under her fingers.

"Oh, Neal," she said, her own chest feeling tight and hopeless.

He stirred, but didn't wake.

Mary got up and went to the fire, which had died down to glowing coals.

Tears blurred her vision, and she nearly put the embers out in her haste to feed in small pieces of driftwood. Finally, though, it was crackling again, flames licking at the rock ring, and Mary had her sobs under some semblance of control.

She knelt by Neal and drew his head gently against her, burying her hands in his ruddy hair.

"You're safe," she murmured. "You're safe with me."

He stirred and muttered, but didn't wake from his restless sleep.

"Neal, listen to me. You have to shift, you have to. I can't heal you, I don't know how. But your wolf can, if you let him."

He didn't snap this time, far too deep in his fever to register her words or fight the idea—but too far, also, to understand the urgency.

Would he die this way, stubbornly resisting his animal form to the very end?

Mary's hands clenched reflexively. She couldn't let that happen.

Neal, she said firmly, without speaking. *Neal!*

There was no answer, just muffled silence behind her closed eyes.

Dammit, Neal, I love you, and I'm not going to let you go like this.

Deeper and deeper she fell into his mind, through fever-crazy dreams and prickling fears.

I won't leave you, she told him.

Then, abruptly, Mary was kneeling in a sunlit plain with no sky, her deer standing beside her. Neal's human form was limp in her arms, ghostly transparent and cool to the touch. She looked for his wolf form, expecting to find it lying nearby in the tall grass.

You have to find him, her deer told her urgently. *They need each other.*

Mary tilted her head back and shouted with all of her strength, "Neal!" It echoed back to her through the strange cavernous space, mockingly. *Neal! Neal!*

As the last echo faded, he came.

Mary had expected him to be injured, as the human self was, but the red maned wolf pranced through the grass on long springy legs, eyes feral and mocking and full —unexpectedly—of anger.

He needs you, she said, and she heard her deer say the same in chorus with her.

He doesn't want me, the wolf said slyly. *He rejects me.*

His look for Neal's ghostly form was full of contempt.

He is hurt, Mary told him. *He will die without you.*

He is weak, the wolf retorted.

You will die without him, Mary's deer said, and she paced in circles through the grass, tossing her delicate head.

I am not weak, the wolf scoffed, and he circled the deer hungrily.

You are angry, said Mary with sudden clarity. *He is not the one who hurt you, but you have no one else left to blame.*

The wolf paused, and the deer put her nose down to touch his in his moment of stillness, fearless and determined.

I can still run, he replied at last.

I can run faster, Mary's deer said gently.

The wolf pulled his lips back in a snarl, but the deer did not back down, keeping her velvety nose against his.

You can heal him, Mary begged, watching Neal's human form fade further and threaten to blow away altogether.

He can heal you, her deer added to the wolf.

The wolf flicked his big ears, staring back into the deer's eyes without words.

Then Neal stirred, and sighed, and said, *Come home.*

Mary woke with a start, her fingers buried in a coarse red mane, not Neal's short hair. She looked down in wonder at the creature lying beside her. He had done it.

Neal had shifted. He had overcome years of trauma and fear and terror and found his way home again.

The red maned wolf still slept, but his breath was strong, and when Mary felt through his fur to his skin, his heartbeat was steady. She wept, exhausted, and buried her face in his fur.

CHAPTER 24

*N*eal woke from dreams of dark-skied sunlight and bones that cracked back into their proper places with blood-chilling sounds. Mary was curled at his side as a deer, head resting against his neck, and it felt comfortable and right, as very little had felt comfortable and right in the last decade.

Looking down at his body, he found that it was not strange or triggering to have paws again, and his wolf was not a painful thorn in his mental side, but a trusted companion once again.

Sunrise was beginning to color the ocean before them, and the tide was out again, revealing a golden-white semi-circle of pristine sand.

He was breathing easily again, he realized, and took a particularly deep experimental inhalation.

It still hurt, and his chest still felt tight, but it was markedly better. His leg had only the barest of aches.

Neal was surprised. He knew how deadly even a partially collapsed lung could be, and while he knew that shifting could heal many ills, he had not expected this level of improvement.

Mary's breath changed and Neal put his nose to hers and gave a grateful, tender lick as she woke.

Her shift to human was seamless and smooth, and Neal wondered if he had ever shifted so gracefully. His own transformation was rockier—he could feel the injured places inside stretch and change as he returned to his human shape. As his body remade itself, it tried to make itself properly, healing the leaking places in his lungs.

"Oh, Neal." Mary was weeping, wrapping her arms around his neck as he rose to gather her up for a close embrace. "I thought I'd lost you."

"I love you," he told her, holding her tightly against him. He still felt weak and slightly dizzy, but the feeling of her skin against his made his strength return. "I love you," he repeated.

She snuggled closer, and Neal could feel her smile against his neck. "I know."

"I'm sorry I was so stubborn," he said sheepishly.

"There you go apologizing again," she teased, but she said it lightly.

I forgive you, his wolf said loftily, as if he'd been the recipient of the apology.

I missed you, he admitted to it, wondering what his response would be.

He got in return a lupine laugh, lolling tongue and all.

"Mmm, you are feeling better," Mary observed, and Neal realized that he had a terrific erection, pressing between them.

"I have lost time to make up for," he said, running a thumb along the slope her neck to her shoulder. "Here we are, lost in the romantic, tropical wilderness, and all I wanted to do was lie in the sand and let you make fire and save us. At the very least, there should have been more snuggling together for warmth."

He followed his thumb with his mouth, kissing to her collarbone, and she hissed in pleasure.

"Will you be very disappointed if I tell you I don't want to just snuggle right now?" she asked slyly.

"I'll take a raincheck," Neal suggested. He didn't stop at her collarbone, but fell to her bountiful breasts, kissing until he had to cough.

"You're still not fully healed," Mary said, drawing back in concern.

"A few more shifts to get everything back into proper shape," Neal guessed, battling his breath back. "But I'm well enough for this." His erection had not ebbed after his coughing fit, and his hands were hungry for Mary's soft skin.

"Maybe you should let me look you over," Mary suggested. When she put her hands on Neal's shoulders, pushed him back down onto the sand and straddled him, he let her.

"You need a proper inspection," she said with a laugh.

First, she kissed him on the mouth, firmly but gently, slowly and with breaks so that he never ran out of air, then started to work her way down his body. Every scratch got a feathery kiss, and spaces between got licks and caresses. She worked her way down his chest, pausing to tease his nipples, and Neal had to draw in a sharp breath as she teased down his abs on a sure course towards the member that was acting as a flagpole below.

"Mmm," she said. "Scratches, bruises. Nothing needs stitches, but this needs a little… attention." Her fingers made a loose loop around his cock, stroking him once from base to tip.

Neal groaned and couldn't quite keep himself from thrusting up at her.

"Uh, uh!" Mary scolded merrily. "Keep still for Nurse Mary, or I'll have to bring in an orderly to tie you down."

Obediently, Neal kept himself still as Mary continued to touch his throbbing member, stroking the skin gently, and scratching tenderly at his balls.

She teased him and tortured him exquisitely, until Neal knew that he was going to lose whatever precious control he had remaining.

"You have to… I'm going to… oh…!"

His pleasure rolled over the top, but Mary had slowed her finger strokes down just enough, to just the correct rate, and he had a moment of sheer bliss without actual release.

While Neal was still reeling from that treatment, marveling at the little miracle, Mary straddled him, bringing her hot, welcoming folds around him.

She was no less gentle riding him than she'd been with her hands, keeping her rhythm slow and deliberate, even as she moaned and clutched fingers through the sand beside them.

When she came, crying out in irresistible pleasure, Neal found a second crest of sensation and lost himself, thrusting back, his own cry of pleasure twining with hers.

CHAPTER 25

*M*ary stretched and laughed, feeling sated and satisfied to the furthest reaches of her toes.

Her stomach rumbled, a reminder her that one part of her, at least, was not in the slightest fulfilled.

"I have a granola bar left," she remembered, springing to find it.

The wrapper had come unsealed at some point, and Mary was dismayed to find a trail of teensy ants inside. At one point, not many days previous, she would have shrieked and thrown it away, but she was hungry, and there weren't that many ants. Mary peeled the granola bar and spent several moments carefully flicking each tiny ant off before she brought it to Neal, who was lying with his hands behind his head, looking up at the clouds skidding through the morning sky.

"I believe they call that a shit-eating grin," Mary said, handing him half of the bar.

Neal accepted half of the bar as he sat up, and Mary was relieved to see that although he winced, he moved easily, and his breaths were deep and steady.

"I cannot wait to get back to the resort and take a shower," she said, squirming. "I have sand in very uncomfortable places.

"We could go for a swim," Neal suggested—though immediately looked trepidatious, probably remembering Mary's near panic-attack from just a few days ago.

It seemed like a very long time ago that Mary had been so afraid of the idea of the ocean, and she found herself looking thoughtfully out at the lapping waves.

"I like the idea," she said, and she looked back at Neal's upraised eyebrows. "I know! I'm as surprised as you are, but after falling down a cliff and sharing a granola bar with ants, I'm up for all kinds of new adventures."

She did insist on putting on her underthings before wading out. "I don't want something swimming up in there," she insisted, at Neal's skeptical look.

He laughed, then teased, "Except me, right?"

Mary laughed back. "Swim on in any time, handsome."

They shared a deep kiss. Mary only pulled away because one of the waves came higher than the others, startling her with a splash of cool water.

Hand in hand, they waded out into the rolling water, and the sand beneath them fell away until they were swimming. Mary was astonished at the clarity of the water and the brilliant blue color of it. She dove down and found shells at the bottom, surfacing with a handful of aquatic treasure.

"Oh, look," she said, sharing the shells with Neal.

He duly admired them, but Mary thought he was really admiring her more; his glance was filled with a tenderness and joy that didn't seemed aimed at the shells she was sharing.

Then one of the shells sprouted legs, and she shrieked

and threw them all away from her. "They have crabs in them still!" she exclaimed, and she was laughing even before they hit the water and began to sink back to the sandy bottom. Neal wrapped his arms around her in comfort, and she giggled weakly against his big shoulder as they half-floated in the water.

"I'm such a ninny," she said apologetically as the adrenaline began to ebb.

"You're not," Neal chided. "Look where you are, what you're doing! You got us firewood in the dark, and ate a granola bar crawling with ants."

"It's easy to be brave for you," Mary said thoughtfully. "You needed me."

Neal's arms tightened around her.

"Besides, I was really hungry," she teased. "And ants are probably good protein."

"I am going to spend the entire afternoon at the buffet when we get back," Neal agreed.

Mary was silent for a moment. "What are we going to do when we get back?" she asked solemnly.

"Buffet," Neal repeated. "All of it, if Chef doesn't stop me."

Mary hit him gently in the arm. "I meant after that. I'm supposed to fly home tomorrow morning."

Neal stilled against her. The waves seemed very loud in his silence.

Mary turned in the circle of his arms so she could look into his face, squinting against the bright sunlight that dazzled off the water at them.

"I love you, Neal, and I think you are well on your way towards healing, but you've got a lot of unfinished business. Your military unit thinks that you're dead, and you have a family who doesn't know what happened to you. You want revenge that you'll probably never get, and even your wolf can't heal everything you've been through."

She watched his face flit through a dozen expressions as he took in her words.

Acceptance was the final look, and Neal drew her close again. "You're right, of course. I have a lot of things to work through, and I don't know how it will all shake out. But if you'll have me…"

"I will," Mary said emphatically.

"… I'll go wherever you are."

"I have a tiny apartment in a tiny town where I have the extra glamorous job of teaching math to middle school students in the throes of puberty. Would you be happy there?"

"I'd be happy anywhere I could be with you." Neal scooped her up and kissed her until they were both dizzy.

"When do you think they'll find us?" Mary asked when they had broken apart, smiling foolishly at each other.

That struck the smile from Neal's face. "Could be late today, or even tomorrow," he surmised. "Travis took the boat to the mainland overnight, so it might be afternoon before they get out on the water, unless they call in for help earlier."

"Could we swim back by ourselves?" Mary suggested nervously. It wasn't as terrifying as she had expected here in the water, and she knew she was a strong swimmer, but the ocean was more alive than any pool she had ever been, and she had no idea how far it would be along the coast to the resort.

Neal considered. "It's a fair way," he said reluctantly. "And there are a few places we'd have to swing out pretty far to avoid rocks. We'd be better off staying where we are and waiting for them to come for us."

Mary smiled slowly, actually pleased by the idea. The

cove, now that Neal was no longer at death's door, was a pleasant little oasis. If they could both shift, they could drink the water from the waterfall, and Mary suspected she could forage for food as a deer, as Neal could as a wolf.

Now that it was sunny and perfect, it was almost better here than at the resort.

Mary's stomach grumbled.

Almost.

CHAPTER 26

*T*hey swam back to shore with easy strokes, pausing to embrace and kiss at lazy intervals, enjoying the sparkle on the water and the musical sound of waves on the shore. As if to apologize for the earlier rain, the day was crystal clear and gorgeous, with just enough of a cool breeze to keep the heat of the sun from being oppressive.

Halfway back, Neal took Mary's arm and pointed.

She squeaked in alarm and clung to him, but gradually relaxed as the turtle under the water swam closer to investigate them and then moved on. A jellyfish got the same reaction, and a school of fish earned only giggles as she swam backwards away from them.

Neal found himself wanting to show her everything. Her excitement and nervousness were adorable, and he loved the way she got past her immediate alarm every time and boldly went forward to new experiences and adventures. She may have considered herself a coward, but she was easily the bravest person Neal had ever known.

When Neal pointed out the whales on the horizon, surfacing and blowing a spray of water up into the air, Mary *ooh*-ed and *ahhh*-ed, and nearly pulled them under in the excitement of spotting one flip its tail above the surface.

He shifted when they gained the land, and he could feel his breath come even easier in wolf form, dark paws dancing the surf. Mary slipped out of her underthings and frolicked beside him in deer form. While she found beach grass to nibble on, he found the scent of some small rodent, which he tracked down to a pile of driftwood and devoured.

He returned to find her trying to coax new flame from her neglected fire, and he cheered her success by lifting her into the air and spinning her around, grateful for strength in his arms once more.

They made love in the sand as the sun moved across the sky into afternoon, and Neal felt like he was discovering her all over again with his own healing body.

The scrapes across her skin had faded to almost nothing, and even the gash along her arm was nothing more than a silver scar now against the deep tan she was developing.

She moved like the ocean under his fingers, rising to his kisses and scratching his shoulders in passion as he entered her.

She was tight and willing at the same time, welcoming and yet deliciously resistant, and Neal wanted to do nothing more than capture the moment forever.

He kept his strokes slow and deliberate, teasing and tantalizing, and bringing her to the brink of pleasure again and again until she was writhing and begging and clawing at him, breathing his name in a way that made his toes clench.

Finally, she came, and Neal couldn't stop his own pleasure at the same time, his release like a triumph.

They lay together, and Neal was deeply grateful for the way his breath went all the way to the bottom of his lungs.

His wolf, grinning in satisfaction within him, was no longer a hated reminder of his trials. He knew that whatever happened, they were partners again.

He rolled over up on one elbow and looked down at Mary, who smiled up at him contentedly.

"You are so amazing," he told her frankly.

She made a funny face. "I have sand in awkward places again," she laughed.

He laughed back at her, and it was as much a delight as breathing again, to open his mouth and hear laughter.

"Do you hear that?" Mary suddenly said, freezing and clutching at his arm.

Over the now familiar roar of the waterfall and the endless lapping of the ocean on the shore, Neal heard a faint, mechanical hum.

"A boat," they said together. Mary fell over herself reaching for her scattered clothing, totally forgetting about the sand she had just complained about.

Neal sprang to his feet without regard for his own nudity, and ran for the beach, desperate to catch the eye of whoever might be out there.

He needn't have worried: if Travis' eagle eyes had not spotted them from the little boat, Bastian suddenly swooping from overhead would not have missed them.

"Shirking your jobs again, are you?" the dragon teased, shifting into human form within a few steps of his neat landing. He was a clothing shifter, so he remained neatly attired in his lifeguard uniform with a first aid kit strapped to his waist.

Neal folded his arms and offered a smile in greeting as

Mary came up to hand him what remained of his tattered clothing.

Travis looked alarmed at her blood-stained shirt, but Mary quickly waved him off. "I'm fine, really. Neal was the one who was hurt."

That earned him a head-to-toe look from Travis.

"I'm fine now," Neal said blithely.

"You should still be looked at," Mary said firmly.

Bastian and Travis exchanged amused looks that would have had Neal gnashing his teeth in irritation just a few days earlier. Now he only shrugged, with a tolerant half-smile.

"Partially collapsed lung," he said off-handedly. "It's better now."

Mary stared at him. "I thought it was just some broken ribs," she said in outrage.

"I didn't want you to worry," Neal said seriously. "There was nothing either of us could do about it."

Mary's eyes were flinty. "I would have appreciated being in the loop anyway."

Neal squirmed under her scrutiny. "How about I put on my clothes and we go back to the resort for a good meal before you read me the riot act."

Travis and Bastian smothered snickers.

"I've got some energy bars," Bastian offered peaceably.

"I've got spare pants," Travis added.

Neal suspected that the boat ride back would have been more uncomfortable if Mary had not been immediately enraptured with the whole affair.

Mindful of her previous fear of boats, he offered her a seat in the middle, but she quickly gravitated towards the edge, looking over the edge at the rippling sea bed below them and squeaking and holding on to him every time that they bounced over a particularly large wave. The resort boat was not the most modern vessel, but it made short work of the journey back to Shifting Sands, and was too loud to allow easy conversation at its top speed.

CHAPTER 27

*M*ary climbed out of the boat onto the dock with a grin. "I want to do that again some-time," she told Neal, as he clambered out behind her and took her hand. She wasn't sure why she had ever been afraid of it. "But maybe a shower first?"

"Then you want to go straight back out on the boat?"

"Then the buffet," she laughed. "For a few hours."

"Yes," Neal agreed merrily.

"Maybe not," Travis cautioned as they walked up the dock to the beach.

Neal sobered with alarming speed, eyes narrow. "What's up?"

Travis glanced at Mary, who tried to look serious and trustworthy back at him. "Beehag's heir Benedict is still here. He brought an... investor."

"Investor?" Neal blinked.

"The investor isn't exactly the savory type, and he's interested in buying the island and ending the lease with the resort. Renegotiating, they're calling it."

Neal whistled. "Scarlet can't be happy about that."

"That's an understatement," Travis agreed. "And that would be tense enough…"

"Do they know about the shifters?" Neal guessed.

"No one is sure," Travis explained. "But these guys are bad news."

"Beehag's nephew didn't fall far from the asshole tree," Neal growled.

"There you go with the understatements again."

Travis paused at the bottom of the steps up from the beach. "It's not an easy time," he cautioned. "Everyone is on edge, and there are a lot of… bodyguards that came with the investors. Armed bodyguards. Creepy, well-armed bodyguards who are not exactly acting respectful of the guests." Travis nodded at Mary. "Especially the female guests," he added apologetically.

Mary felt Neal's hand tense in hers.

"Probably mercenaries," Neal guessed from the description. "Have there been any incidents?"

"Nothing worse than leering," Travis said, to Mary's relief. "But it could get awkward if they said the wrong thing to Magnolia and she took offense. On the upside, Virginia finally put on clothes and stopped draping herself over the furniture like meat."

"That's a sign of dire times," Neal observed dryly.

The walk up the numerous steps from the beach to the pool deck that had Mary blushing with memories took very little time, and they abruptly came to the top of the stairs to find a collection of people having a heated discussion.

Beehag's heir, Benedict, Mary guessed, was the greasy, scrawny youth—he looked barely old enough to be admitted to the resort, and he was scowling defensively.

Scarlet was looking at him like he was some kind of small worm, and lesser men than he would have squirmed the way he was.

"We have a contract," Scarlet was hissing, and Mary guessed by her fists that she was keeping herself tightly in control. "It has clauses for breach."

"My lawyer assures me that everything about this transaction is completely legal," Benedict whined. "There's a more than generous severance fee."

Scarlet was clearly unimpressed by the figure they were offering her, though Benedict seemed to think it ought to assuage her ire.

She turned her icy attention to the investor. "There are other resorts for sale. More accessible locations."

"There are no other resorts like *this* one," the investor replied with a chuckle. "Shifting Sands has several unique properties that appeal to me particularly."

The mercenaries, were, true to the warnings, looming figures, each of them easily the size of Neal and armed with wicked-looking guns. Mary glanced at Scarlet and back at them. She didn't think that Scarlet was actually afraid of any of them, but considered herself unpleasantly bound by the contract.

The investor was wearing a suit and standing with his back to the party coming up the stairs, and he turned to glance at them with an unconcerned, sleazy smile.

In an instant, everything shifted.

Neal's hand in Mary's became an anchor, wrapping around her fingers even more tightly than before, as he hissed, "Lewis…"

CHAPTER 28

*N*eal did an automatic assessment of the situation as they crested the stairs, taking stock of the bodyguards—six bruisers—and the other figures standing there. The bodyguards looked bored, but professional; Neal knew at once that he had been correct about guessing they were mercenaries by the way they were subtly assessing each other as well as the newcomers, fingers lazy on their weapons. He dismissed Benedict as a useless youth with too high an estimation of himself and no physical skills. He knew better than to discount Scarlet as an asset, though he had to lump her into a total unknown category.

The figure with his back to them was the most intriguing. The suit was clearly fine quality and perfectly tailored, and the body beneath was unexpectedly large and powerful. From the expense of his dress, Neal guessed he had to be one of the investors.

Then, he turned, and Neal saw his face.

Lewis recognized Neal in the same moment that Neal realized who was standing at the top of the stairs and, with a gesture, directed all of the mercenary attention on him. Weapons that had been held loosely were at ready. The men that had looked the laziest were suddenly sharp-eyed and alert.

"Mr. Byrne," the drug lord said in oily tones, turning all of his attention from Scarlet to Neal. "How… pleasant to see you again."

Neal forced a smile onto his face. "I wish I could say that that was mutual, Lewis."

Scarlet glanced from one to the other, frowning thoughtfully, but said nothing.

Mary's hand in his tightened, and Neal wished her anywhere else as Lewis' glance turned from him to her.

As polite as could be, Lewis offered his hand to Mary. "My dear," he said slickly. "How lovely to meet you. Mr. Byrne is an… old friend."

"I, uh, I'm Mary North," Mary said in a quavering voice. She had to reluctantly let go of Neal and very tentatively shook his hand. It didn't escape anyone's notice that he held onto it a little longer than she wanted him to.

"I wouldn't say friend," Neal ground out, holding his anger tightly in check.

Lewis gave a toothy smile. "No need to be pedantic. Business associates, if you'd prefer?"

"My mission was to kill you," Neal said flatly.

Mary's breath hissed in alarm, and Neal could feel the air around Scarlet chill. Behind him, at the top of the steps, Travis shuffled his feet and Bastian flexed his hands. Benedict sweated in the muggy air.

"Fun times," Lewis laughed. "But come now, you aren't even considered alive by your old unit. Surely we can put a failed mission behind us."

"Not when the failed mission was to take down a turncoat drug lord who hid behind school children." Neal's wolf growled from his throat.

"There's no reason to escalate this," Lewis said smoothly, turning away from Neal to address Scarlet. "We simply need to finalize the paperwork"

"What am I supposed to tell the guests?" Scarlet asked. Neal immediately found the calmness of her voice deeply suspicious.

"That they should have purchased travel insurance," Benedict suggested with a snigger.

Lewis shot Benedict a squelching look that silenced the laugh mid-breath. "The resort is simply changing ownership. The staff has their jobs, if they want them, and the guests are welcome to stay for the remainder of their reservation. I'm sure you'll understand why I will insist having *you* escorted off the island, Ms. Stanson."

"Of course," Scarlet said, ice in her voice.

Neal wondered what Lewis knew about Scarlet that the rest of them didn't.

CHAPTER 29

"*A*nd you, Ms. North," Lewis said, turning back to her.

Mary startled, and clung to Neal's hand.

"I'm sure you understand our desire to keep things from escalating."

Mary, keenly aware of everyone's attention, squeaked, "Yes. Of course."

Lewis smiled at her. "Than I'm sure you won't mind coming with us. As assurance of peaceful resolution."

Neal's hand threatened to cut off circulation in Mary's fingers and Mary's world went white with terror. Go with these frightful men and their gigantic guns?

Lewis continued, talking directly to Neal now. "I know that you are debating whether or not to shift, and trying to decide whether or not you could get to my throat before bullets could get to her." He glanced over their shoulders. "And you, you're trying to decide if being in dragon form would intimidate my men. I assure you, it would not. I've generously offered you your jobs. But unemployment doesn't need to be the worst of your problems."

Mary heard Bastian shift his weight on his feet behind them.

"We can draw up the necessary paperwork in my office," Scarlet said coldly. "And I'm sure you won't mind if I pack a few of my things."

Lewis nodded. "I appreciate keeping things... civilized." He put a hand imperiously out to Mary and snapped his fingers.

Mary felt Neal's growl rather than heard it.

No, Neal! Mary said wordlessly at him.

She wasn't sure if the speech would work in human form, but he stilled, and let her step away from him.

He won't hurt me if we all do as he says, she tried to reassure him, not entirely convinced herself.

A wordless wave of deep skepticism and reluctant acceptance was the only thing returned to her.

Trembling, Mary put her hand in Lewis' and he tucked it into his elbow as he turned away, pulling her forward.

She had time to give Neal one quick goodbye glance, hoping she looked brave rather than simply terrified, and then they were climbing the resort steps past the bar towards Scarlet's hilltop office.

Benedict looked between the mercenaries who dropped behind at Lewis' gesture and the party making the climb, then dashed to catch up with Lewis.

CHAPTER 30

$\mathcal{W}$atching Mary walk away with Scarlet on one side and Lewis capturing her hand on the other was one of the hardest things Neal had ever done. His wolf snarled helplessly inside him and for once, they were in reluctant harmony.

"Well," Travis said, coming up on one side. "That answers the question of whether they know we're shifters or not.

Two of Lewis' hard-faced men had been left behind, assault rifles at hand. They clearly expected to be feared, and that gave Neal an idea.

"You don't mind if I sit, do you?" he asked casually, and he sank down into one of the lounge chairs without waiting for their answer.

He smiled, delighting in the way the mercenaries shifted on their feet and kept their faces carefully stony. It was never comfortable knowing that your enemy wasn't taking you seriously.

"Lewis always had one fatal flaw," he said cheerfully, leaning back into a deck chair, looking for all the world as if he had nothing better to do than lounge in the sun over-looking the pool while his mate was hauled off as a hostage.

Travis and Bastian exchanged brief, mystified looks, but played along willingly, pulling up their own chairs.

"What's that?" Travis asked, swinging his feet up on the lounge and settling his sunglasses over his eyes.

Bastian picked up a magazine, hamming it up even further.

"He always underestimated shifters," Neal said merrily. "Like, he didn't know about the other things we can do."

It was the mercenaries' turn to exchange looks, and Travis immediately caught Neal's intentions.

"He doesn't know we can turn invisible?"

"He doesn't know a thing about that," Neal agreed. "I bet he even thinks the silver bullet thing is a myth and thinks that those standard bullets would stop us." He nodded at the gun the nearest mercenary was holding in what were now white-knuckled hands.

The second mercenary made a skeptical noise, and when the shifters looked at him, broke his cold facade to scoff, "You wouldn't be saying those things with us listening if it were true."

Bastian laughed lightly. "We'll just use a forget-me field on you… if we let you leave at all."

"Because really," Travis added swiftly. "How do you think shifters have stayed a secret this long without those extra tricks?"

The first mercenary scowled at his partner. "Quit talking to them, Jake."

Out of the corner of Neal's eyes, a flash of movement caught his attention. The gazelle was browsing on the lawn by the deck—suspiciously close, for her.

Jake, defying the other's suggestion, mockingly said,

"You wouldn't have let Lewis walk off with your girlfriend if you could have stopped him."

Touché, Neal thought, scrambling for a cool response through the flare of anger at the memory of Mary's last fearful glance.

"Didn't have to stop them," Travis said, before Neal could think of anything. "They're walking right into Scarlet's trap, after all. Mary's safe as houses with her."

How safe are *houses?* Neal had to wonder, and he would have shot Travis a grateful look if he hadn't been concentrating on appearing cool and in control of the situation.

Jake's partner hooked him by the elbow and pulled him out of easy earshot, toward the lawn where the gazelle was still pretending to graze so they could exchange whispers.

Neal kept a practiced eye on their weapons, judging how they were held.

Bastian nudged a shoulder towards them and raised his eyebrows, subtly asking Neal if they should try to take them by surprise. Neal concealed his head shake by raking fingers through his hair lazily. Whatever else these soldiers were, they were professionals, and their attention was complete enough that their weapons could be brought to bear before the shifters could take them down. They looked rattled, but not entirely distracted, glancing around often.

At a moment when they weren't watching him, Neal gave a wave to the gazelle, who was still grazing in earshot. He wasn't quite sure what she could do to help them, but another source of distraction would give them more options.

The gazelle lifted her head and with slow, cautious steps, walked to where the men stood with their guns.

At her first deliberate steps, the guards were at full attention, discussion over whether to call Lewis and warn him about the supposed trap at a standstill. Jake lifted the muzzle of his gun to point at her, while the other had his rifle down, but a finger at the trigger, swapping his attention between the gazelle and the shifters lounging on the pool deck.

She scented the air as she walked forward, one slow hoof after another. Jake lowered his gun, dismissing her as a threat; despite the long, spiraled horns, she was very small and delicate looking. Then she riveted all of their attention—and Neal's as well—as she rippled and shifted.

A woman knelt there, shrouded in waves of waist-length hair in mixed black and white. At first glance, she was an old woman, the white in her hair and the gauntness of her limbs giving an impression of age. But her face, though haunted, was free of wrinkles, and her eyes were wide and full of youthful innocence as she looked up through her hair at them.

"You are bad men," she said chidingly.

She had all of their attention, much more than she ought to, and it took Neal a moment to shake off her spell himself and realize that the soldiers' hands had gone slack on their guns.

He rose to his feet, waiting for either of the body-guards' attention to snap back to him at the sound of the lounge chair creaking underneath him. He poked Travis, who blinked stupidly at him for a moment before turning to put an elbow in Bastian's side.

Bastian actually pinched himself to complete his release from the gazelle's hypnotic spell.

Neal rushed forward, realizing that this chance wouldn't last forever, and Bastian and Travis followed him into action.

Taking the weapons from the men was laughably easy; they didn't even startle until the shoulder straps were released and the gazelle was leaping away in her antelope form again. They blinked stupidly at Neal and Travis, but it didn't take a lot of time to convince them they were beaten. They gradually shook their heads and put their hands up, scowling.

CHAPTER 31

*M*ary looked from Lewis to Scarlet as they walked into the courtyard that opened onto Scarlet's office and personal quarters, glanced at Benedict and the men with the guns, and then turned her attention back to the most important two.

Scarlet's face was a perfect mask, utterly impenetrable, but Mary could feel the anger sparking off of her, and knew beyond a shadow of a doubt that the woman had no actual intention of turning her resort over to these men. Neal's revelation that Lewis was a criminal had changed the transaction for her, turning it from something inevitable that she would have to accept to a battle she was bracing herself to fight.

Lewis must have sensed the same thing Mary did.

"There's no reason to make any of this unpleasant," he said, voice silky, but threatening. "You know that you don't have a choice in the matter. It's all quite legal and above board, and no one needs to get hurt if we do it the easy way."

Mary bit back a squeak as one of the mercenaries pointed his rifle more obviously at her.

"Take only what you need, I will have my men pack the rest to ship to you on the mainland within a week's time. I assure you I pay them well enough that they won't be interested in your belongings."

"You aren't going to just let us leave," Scarlet said, her own voice chilly and skeptical.

Lewis chuckled. "*You* may, lady, and any of your staff that chooses to go. It's quite true that I can't leave Neal free to tell tales."

Mary startled, and sudden terror for Neal overwhelmed her own fears.

"But you owe him nothing," Lewis continued smoothly to Scarlet. "Our history is none of your concern, and you can preserve the remainder of your staff and take advantage of our very generous monetary offer simply by using a little good judgment."

Scarlet's face betrayed nothing as she turned to walk into her office, but Lewis stopped her anyway.

"No, I think you should not go into there yourself," Lewis suggested, and he looked to the closest and burliest of the mercenaries with a question on his brow.

He got a surprisingly toothy smile in return, and a nod. "This is one of the strong places, one of the places of power," the man said.

His words crystallized something that had been bothering at the back of Mary's mind. Scarlet's office had always left her feeling unsettled, but the mercenary's words made her recognize that it wasn't Scarlet herself, but something deeper and older, something asleep beneath the resort. She felt like a more powerful shifter here, and she suddenly wondered how much of a role that power had played in Neal's swift recovery.

"No surprises," Lewis warned, and all of the mercenaries felt so tightly wound that Mary expected them to snap.

"It's not a power that can be controlled," Scarlet said, her voice full of warning.

"You mean *you* can't control it," Lewis scoffed.

"I mean it doesn't like to be controlled," Scarlet said softly. "If you wake it, I don't think it will appreciate either you or your actions."

"That's a risk I'm willing to take."

Mary felt adrift, like a child listening to a conversation that adults were having, understanding their words, but not their meaning. Benedict looked nervous, and Mary caught him crossing his fingers superstitiously.

Scarlet went into her office with the bodyguard and carefully gathered a few things—a handful of files and a laptop were tucked into a rolling bag, and she picked up an unadorned wooden box, all under the scrutiny of the watchful bodyguard and Lewis, who stood with his arms crossed, watching through the door.

"Let's see you off in the Jeep then," Lewis said, almost merrily. He seemed to think that Scarlet's quiet was a sign of her defeat, but Mary strongly suspected otherwise. "Our plane is waiting at the airstrip to take you back to the mainland."

They walked through the courtyard, two mercenaries in the front, and two trailing. Lewis, still holding Mary's hand at his elbow walked behind Scarlet and Benedict.

Benedict was babbling something like an apology to Scarlet. "I'm sure you understand. The offer was just too good. I couldn't turn it down…"

No one paid him any mind.

CHAPTER 32

*N*eal left the mercenaries well-wrapped in duct tape, disarming them of an array of knives and small weapons first.

"We're outnumbered," Neal said as the shifters climbed the steps to the bar deck. "We've only got these two guns against five of them." He automatically discounted Benedict Beehag as a combatant, but he was not foolish enough to think that Lewis was not still in prime fighting form, whether he had traded his fatigues for suits or not.

"And a dragon," Bastian reminded him, flexing his shoulders but not shifting. "Two guns and a *dragon*. That counts for something."

"Beehag had a tranquilizer that changed shifters back to human," Neal cautioned. "We have to assume that Benedict has given that formula to Lewis."

Bastian scowled, but nodded.

"Hey Tex," Travis called into the bar. "Want to join a reckless, doomed rescue mission?"

"What are we rescuing?" Tex asked with a lazy drawl, not putting down the towel he was drying glasses with.

"His mate," Travis answered, jerking a thumb at Neal.

"Scarlet," Bastian added.

"Shifting Sands," Neal finished gravely.

"You had me at reckless and doomed," Tex said, grinning. He put the glass away carefully and came out from behind the bar.

"Would Graham…?" Neal started.

As if summoned, the landscaper materialized from the back entrance to the bar, a wicked machete in one hand. He didn't offer an explanation, but Neal had to guess that he had spotted the strange party headed for Scarlet's office and recognized that something was afoot.

At his heels, was Breck, still in his waitstaff uniform, but looking uncharacteristically grim-faced.

"These are starting to feel like better odds," Travis said confidently. "I can get Magnolia, she's a polar bear who's good to have in a fight, and where she goes, Chef goes."

"I can keep them from being able to leave," Breck offered. "It wouldn't take much to disable the Jeep." At Neal's nod, he trotted away with the grace and speed of his leopard.

"They still have more ranged weapons," Neal cautioned. "And hostages. We need a plan. And a backup plan." He set his jaw. "I'll need your phone, Tex."

The list in his pocket had long since dissolved to unreadable, but Neal didn't need it. He dialed Major Washburn's number as if he'd always known it.

"This had better be good," Judy answered, her voice painfully familiar even after ten years.

Neal could hear the whine of engines in the background, and guessed she was at an airport.

"Judes," he said roughly, and he walked across the bar for whatever privacy he could get.

There was a moment of silence at the other end of the line. "Who the hell *is* this? How did you get this number?"

Neal recognized the deep thrum that underlay the airplane engines. A carrier. The team was somewhere on the flight deck of a carrier. But what ocean? Were they close enough?

"Judes," he said again. "Listen up, I need a support team at the coordinates of this phone. I've got Lewis, but don't have the resources to hold him myself. There are civilians at stake." *My mate*, he didn't say.

"Lewis? What the—Neal, is that *you?*"

"It's me," Neal assured her, and it was odd to realize that he meant it. He felt more like himself than he had in ten years. He was alive again, and on the hunt. His feet were on solid ground, his wolf was in alignment with him, and he had purpose.

"Where the hell have you been? It's been ten fucking years, you jack—"

"It's a long story," Neal cut her off. "A really long story. And I promise I'll split a bottle and tell you the whole damn thing, but not now. I need the team. Lewis has at least four bodyguards, moderately armed, and two hostages …"

Without waiting for her agreement, he detailed the basic lay of the resort and Lewis' resources.

"I don't know how fast we can get there," Judy said when he was finally done. "These things need approval from upstairs."

"Damn," Neal laughed. "It's been longer than I thought if you're waiting for approval these days. Aren't you a general yet?"

"When you hit colonel they start making you write your own fucking reports," Judy groused.

"You haven't changed a bit," Neal laughed. He sobered quickly. "Come as fast as you can. I have to go."

He knew that Lewis wouldn't wait docilely for the team to arrive, and his mate was at stake.

CHAPTER 33

*T*hey were standing by the Jeep, waiting as the driver poked under the hood, cursing and casting nervous glances at Lewis.

Scarlet was so tightly coiled that Mary didn't feel safe standing next to her, but a quick glance showed the red-headed woman looking utterly serene, her laptop case in one easy hand, the box tucked under the other arm. Every strand of her hair was in place.

Her crimson hair reminded Mary of Neal's and she shifted on her feet, worried sick. They hadn't heard any shots, and surely she would know if her mate had been unceremoniously dispatched.

As if in response to the idea, she heard Neal's voice in her head.

Mary…?

She looked down, letting the curtain of her dirty hair cover her face.

Neal? Are you all right? Lewis says he's going to… She stopped herself, trying to rein in the hysteria that came with even the idea.

We're free, he replied quickly, with a rush of comfort like a caress. *We're* fine. *Can you make a diversion?*

"Oh!" she said out loud, and that got her the attention of the two guards.

"Is there a problem?" Lewis asked sharply.

Mary squirmed, realizing that as diversions went, this wasn't well thought out. "I, ah, just realized that my flight is in just a few hours. I'm probably going to miss it, and I won't be able to re-book unless I call in advance."

Lewis looked disgusted.

Mary set her jaw. "Maybe an airline flight doesn't mean that much to you," she said with pepper. "But I'm a math teacher, and I saved up a seriously long time for those airline miles."

She had their attention, but not all of it.

"You may be some big-shot millionaire jungle gigolo, but some of us work for a living!" Exhaustion and adrenaline made her feel jittery and hollow, but Mary dredged down to try to recall the worst of her students' dramatic fits. "This isn't fair!" she wailed, and she stomped her foot and set her hands on her hips.

"I saved all my money for years to come to this place, and all I got was marooned in the wilderness and kidnapped! This was supposed to be a lush vacation, and it's been horrible and it's not fair!"

The effect must have been ridiculous, with her unwashed hair, crusty from saltwater, and her ripped, blood-stained clothing, but it had the desired result: she had the attention of all of the guards, and even Scarlet was staring at her as if she'd lost her mind.

"I need to make a phone call," she whined. "You have to let me call the airline, *right now.*"

When they glanced at each other, clearly not sure what

to do with her, Mary stomped her foot again. "It's not fair!" she shrieked, and burst into noisy tears.

"Oh, give her a phone," Lewis said in disgust, and after a moment, Benedict dug out a shiny modern smartphone, unlocked it with his thumbprint, and handed it to her.

Mary sniffed, and made a great show of wiping her tears away. "Can anyone get the phone number for Costa Rican Air?" she whined after a moment of fiddling with it, waving the phone around. "I can't seem to get data on this one."

One of the mercenaries pulled out his own smartphone. "I'm detecting wireless on this, but I need the passcode."

Scarlet, still inscrutable, shrugged. "I'd have to check my log—I change it every week."

Another guard pulled out his own smartphone. "I've got a bar of data, wait, no, I've lost it."

"You could just call information," a third suggested.

"I've let this fall asleep," Mary said sweetly, handing the phone back to Benedict. "You'll have to unlock it again."

The timer she had discretely set to a ringtone went off just as he took it, and he almost dropped it, then fumbled trying to figure out how to answer it. "What the hell?!"

"I don't know!" Mary said defensively, using her very best clueless student voice. "It's your phone!"

"For fuck's sake," Lewis snarled. "Is the goddamn Jeep fixed yet?"

They all looked towards the driver, to find him slumped on the ground. Tex stood beside the Jeep, a baseball bat in his hands. A leopard was crouched beside him.

"You know you shouldn't drive and use your phone at the same time," Neal chided from behind them.

Mary's heart lifted to see him, holding a gun in steady hands, training it on Lewis. Travis was to one side with another large gun, and Graham was flanking the guards on the other, a machete held grimly in one hand; one of the guards was lying at his feet. Behind him, a massive pair of bears, one a polar bear, one a giant grizzly, were growling.

The remaining bodyguards reacted quickly, re-pocketing their phones smoothly and regaining their grips on their weapons. But Lewis was faster than any of them, and before Mary could react, she was being held against him by her wrists, a handgun at her forehead. Beside her, one of the guards did the same with Scarlet.

"You didn't think this out well," Lewis sneered, and Mary wanted to agree.

A giant, dark shape passed overhead and landed with a deep thump on their far side, green wings like vast sails folding into jeweled sides. *A dragon*. Mary could only see it in her peripheral vision, but she could see the reaction in the mercenaries: fear and uncertainty.

Well, she could relate.

CHAPTER 34

*I*t was a standoff, at best. The two forces were evenly matched, in Neal's estimation, and Lewis had hostages. He was smart about it, too—holding Mary where Neal couldn't get a shot at him without risking her too. It did, however, mean that his back was to a dragon. Neal was sure that was worth something. He kept his sights trained on Lewis, and knew that he just needed to keep him talking until an opportunity presented itself, or backup arrived.

Patience, he reminded himself. He concentrated on keeping his breath steady, and his shot clean.

A week ago, he wouldn't have been able to hold the gun without shaking, he realized. He wouldn't have been centered enough to get this far. He'd probably have done something stupid and suicidal already, and risked Mary's life as well.

A week ago, he'd been a different man.

"You're getting sloppy, Lewis," he said gravely. If Lewis was talking, he wasn't shooting, and Neal had backup on the way. "Last time we tried this, you had a tranq dart waiting for me."

"I didn't think you'd survive in Beehag's cage," Lewis scoffed. "I'm surprised you're alive. Your team doesn't think you are. I'm sorry, that's your *ex*-team, of course. The funeral was lovely, according to my man on the inside."

Neal set his teeth. Lewis had someone on the team? Cold fire ran through his veins. Was it Judy? Was the backup he had planned in vain?

He couldn't let any of that show in his voice. "Might have known you had someone from the team in your pocket. Is it Remmy? Gobber?" He didn't add Judy to the list.

Lewis seemed confident that he had the upper hand. "It's amazing what power money has. Especially when family is involved. Especially family who's sick and needs the kind of care only money can buy."

Neal dredged into his memory. Remmy's sister had gone through cancer treatment, not long before their fateful last mission together. She hadn't had insurance that would cover it, and Remmy had been worried... and then strangely unconcerned not long after.

"So, it's Remmy." Neal shrugged. "That's not much of an infiltration."

"You've been out of the loop," Lewis reminded him. "Remmy's not just the comms guy now, he's second in command."

They'd given a traitor his position? Neal had to rein in his temper, and wondered suddenly if Lewis was playing him. Whatever else Lewis was, he *was* clever.

The idea steadied him. "You know much about your boss?" he asked, raising his voice to carry further to the bodyguards standing around them. "You're new hires, don't you wish you knew what kind of circus he was planning to drag you into? And did you ever wonder what happened to his last crew?"

Though he kept his gaze through the sight of his gun on Lewis, he could feel the barb hit home. A few of the younger mercenaries shifted their feet and Neal knew they were listening.

"Lewis offers a lot of money for loyalty," Neal continued derisively. "You're probably thinking that it's worth what he's paying for a little danger. But Lewis really hates to pay his bills, and since he's a traitor himself, he doesn't trust anyone else either. It's funny, what a mortality rate his mercenaries have. Usually *after* the danger has past."

They were all listening to him now, and Lewis was scowling. He shifted Mary in his grasp, effectively keeping her between Neal and himself.

Lewis' phone gave a sudden blurble, and he carefully reached down to check it. A toothy smile spread across his face. "Speaking of turncoats," he said cheerfully. "I guess your team is on its way now. Cleverly done, Byrne. Too bad that they won't get here in time."

Mary gave a squeak as Lewis tightened his grip on her.

Neal fought down his urge to act and reminded himself to be patient, to wait. "You don't need Plan B if Plan A is still going well," he bluffed cheerfully. He pitched his voice to the mercenaries. "We won't hurt anyone who surrenders. You have to ask yourself which party you think is going to end up treating you with more humanity—the resort staff of animal shifters, or the turncoat who relies on people betraying their friends and hides behind women and children when things get tough."

Mercenaries tended to have a code of honor, and it

often excluded using civilians as hostages—especially children. The fact that Lewis was using two apparently defenseless women now played well into Neal's speech.

Behind Lewis, the dragon shifted his wings and growled, and Lewis turned to glance at him, finally offering the shot that Neal had been waiting for as his finger relaxed from the trigger of the gun at Mary's head.

As tempting as it was to put a bullet in Lewis' forehead, Neal took the harder, more humane shot, right through the arm holding the gun.

Lewis howled, dropping the gun as Mary spun out of his grasp and sensibly dropped to the ground with her hands over her head.

Neal heard his own shot in that crazy moment, and Bastian's dragon roar, and another several rounds being fired. He didn't see what happened to Scarlet, but heard a crunch of breaking bones and glanced to find the guard falling away from her, shrieking in pain and cradling his gun arm.

Then Neal was driving forward, leaping over Mary to tackle Lewis and bring him to the ground. He heard howls and grunts and more ear-splitting shots as the rest of the staff took on the remaining mercenaries who hadn't been swayed by his speech, but he focused on Lewis, who was reaching with his off hand for his dropped gun.

"I don't think so," Neal said firmly, and smashed him in the face with the butt of the assault rifle he was still holding, taking cathartic delight in watching Lewis' eyes roll up in his head.

The sounds of fighting died out quickly, and Neal looked around to find Tex relieving the last guard of his weapons. Graham's mercenary was on the ground, whimpering and holding his hands up for mercy. Bastian was human again, looking disappointed at not having anyone left to fight, and Benedict was cowering against the car with his hands over his ears being completely ignored. Magnolia was back in her human form, brushing her flowered dress back into shape as Chef picked up her wide white hat.

Graham had been grazed with one of the wild shots, and Bastian offered to clean it up. Graham looked down at the blood oozing down his shoulder and shrugged, wincing. "It'll heal," he said.

"You all right, Scarlet?" Travis asked.

"He missed," she answered calmly, smoothing her blouse and tucking a strand of artistically loose hair back.

Neal wasn't sure if he believed her or not.

"Oh, Neal," Mary said, uncovering her ears. "You saved us!"

Neal gathered her up into his arms, holding her tight. "I owed you one."

She wrapped her arms around him, and Neal could have sat there and held onto her forever.

Tex cleared his throat. "What do you want us to do with these guys?" he asked.

Neal reluctantly let go of Mary and helped her to her feet.

Scarlet was scowling at Benedict. "You've certainly laid a mess of trouble at our door," she said coldly. "I presume that the sale is off and you'll be cleaning this up?"

Benedict opened one eye and looked up at her. "Oh. Um, yes. I'll be calling my lawyer immediately and canceling the whole thing. I didn't know he was a... a... drug lord or whatever."

Neal snapped his fingers at Benedict. "I need to make a phonecall first."

Benedict obediently handed it over.

"Are you getting any bars of data?" Mary asked merrily.

Neal had to stop laughing before he could dial the phone to warn Judy about Remmy.

CHAPTER 35

*W*hile Neal stepped away to make his phone call, Mary felt like the weight of the past few days was suddenly upon her. She became intensely aware of how dirty and tired and hungry she felt, and how ragged and stained her clothing was.

Scarlet, by comparison, still looked like she'd just stepped out of a salon.

"You are welcome to stay longer at the resort," she offered. "If you can change your plane tickets, I will give you another week in the cottage at no charge. Your Shifting Sands experience should not be so heavy on surviving in the wilderness and being held hostage."

"I'd like that," Mary said with a weary laugh. "But right now I'd mostly like a shower and about four hours at the buffet."

Scarlet laughed with her, and Mary thought it was unexpectedly genuine sounding. There was relief in her face, and Mary realized that she hadn't just been angry about losing Shifting Sands and being shuffled off the island. She'd been afraid.

It was somehow comforting to know that there were things that someone like Scarlet was afraid of, too.

"We'll leave the staff to clean this up," Scarlet suggested. "And I'll need to add duct tape to my list of supplies to reorder."

Mary watched Scarlet go off, waiting for Neal to finish his phone call.

He came back with a familiar dark scowl on his face. It lightened when he caught sight of Mary again, and he bent to give her a lingering kiss.

"We've got this," Bastian said, waving them off. The mercenaries were being neatly trussed and completely disarmed, and marched off to… Mary didn't care where. She assumed that they would be kept until the Costa Rican authorities could get there, and was just as happy to look forward to the promised shower.

"I still have sand in awkward places," she told Neal. "My cottage?"

He took her hand and walked beside her down the steps. The sun was making its wild lunge into the ocean for sunset, and everything was cast in golden light. The few clouds near the horizon were fuchsia and orange, and the ocean made its siren song over the sounds of birds and insects.

The smells wafting from the dining hall almost made them turn in their tracks.

"A very fast shower," Mary said, despite the grumbling of her stomach.

"A very fast one," Neal agreed.

That vow lasted only as long as it took to stagger to Mary's cottage and strip each other out of their clothing.

She could not keep her hands from the planes of his muscles, and although she got the shower started and pulled him in after her, soaping herself seemed like a terrible use of her time when she could be kissing him, and letting him caress her and lift her up onto the bench with her legs eagerly spread.

He entered her, slick and shamelessly inviting, and Mary had to bite back cries of pleasure and peaking desire.

"Don't, don't stop," she begged in his ear, nibbling at his neck and clutching at those amazing broad shoulders.

"Don't let go," he told her back, lifting her effortlessly along the wall to get her into a position where he could thrust easily into her, over and over again until she was drowning in pleasure and her begging was incoherent.

Then he was coming too, thrusting with increasingly urgent strokes until he made an animal noise near Mary's ear and then coursed into her with his seed.

They stood slowly as they regained control of their breath and the waves of their pleasure ebbed away. Neal knocked a bottle of shampoo off the rack and caught it deftly, but not before it had spilled onto Mary's shoulder.

"Close," she said, scooping it up and redepositing it on her head.

After that, the shower was more utilitarian, but if Mary lingered a little longer than was strictly necessary in some spots while lathering Neal with soap then it was understandable, and he certainly didn't object.

CHAPTER 36

*N*eal felt like a new man. Showered, dressed in clothing that (mostly) fit, and sitting across from Mary in the open dining hall, it seemed like it had been more than just a few scant hours since they'd been rescued from their private cove. It seemed insane that they'd been taken as hostages and rescued themselves in that time, and Neal still found it hard to believe that Lewis—Lewis that he'd been sent to bring down ten years ago—was in custody.

"How does it feel?" Mary asked quietly.

Their plates were empty between them, though they'd been refilled several times.

Scarlet had insisted that the staff be served in the restaurant, and Breck, Bastian, Travis, and Tex were regaling a rapt audience with a version of the situation that Neal suspected had little resemblance to the actual events.

Neal shrugged, not sure what Mary was asking about.

"Lewis is why you went to Beehag's prison," she reminded him. "Does it feel like closure to finally capture him?"

Neal frowned, trying to pinpoint why he didn't feel vindicated. "Not exactly," he said thoughtfully.

"Did you really set Benedict's phone to ring when you handed it back?" Breck called across the dining room, interrupting them.

Mary laughed, looking up at him. "I just set a timer," she explained with a shy shrug. "Anything to be disruptive."

"Honey, you are a mastermind," Breck said with approval. "Let me bring you guys dessert."

Despite having polished off several plates of Chef's braised pork cutlets and tender vegetables with red potato wedges, Mary and Neal both accepted the tall, fluffy slices of angel food cake smothered in fresh berries and whipped cream.

Neal was chasing the last blueberry across his plate when he heard the distant sound of chopper blades, and his restlessness finally made sense.

It was several moments before Mary noticed it, and Neal spent those moments watching her face as she savored the last morsels of her cake.

"What is that?" she finally said, listening.

"That was Plan B," Neal said cryptically. At her quizzical look, he explained. "That's my old team. I called them as soon as we got free of the first group of guards. You're hearing a heavy helicopter, just a few minutes out."

Mary's eyes grew wide, but she took that as beautifully in stride as she had their entire adventure.

"How does *that* feel?"

It was a valid question, and one that Neal didn't have an answer for, even when they were standing together at the parking area at the top of the resort outside the gates— the only clear, level place at the resort with space for a landing.

Mary stood close beside him, clinging to his hand. Though he suspected that it was for her own comfort, he took an equal amount of strength from it. She shielded her eyes as the helicopter whirled to a landing, but Neal just squinted at it in the darkness. Judy would be using radar to make the landing, and she must know that he was already there, waiting at a safe range by the entrance.

Watching his team exit the lit helicopter was odd, the familiar shapes of their shoulders beneath the armor they were wearing; the way they each moved and held their weapons; and the other, more subtle differences that weren't apparent until they stepped into the light by the gate.

Judy had dyed her hair a deep nut brown and let it grow out a few inches more than Neal had ever expected she would, almost to her shoulders. Gobber still had no hair, and refused to wear a helmet except to battle, but he had more years of wrinkles in his face, and there was a new scar by his ear. Jessy was still tiny and fast, but had braids in her black hair now, and a stiff motion that suggested a healing shoulder injury.

Remmy—Neal's gut clenched. Remmy still had that too-young look, as red-headed as Neal was, but twice as freckled, with big innocent eyes in his round face. When Neal met his gaze, Remmy flinched so quickly Neal almost doubted that he'd seen it, but when he looked at Judy, he knew at once that she had seen it too, and that it was the last confirmation she'd been waiting for.

She gave a quick, professional gesture, and Thomas, who was giant and umber-skinned and hadn't aged a day, was swiftly behind Remmy, disarming him with practiced hands before Remmy could even blink. Jessy lowered her weapon in a not so subtle way, keeping it trained on Remmy.

"You got here fast," Neal said, not wanting to comment on the action, even as Remmy started to protest, "What's going on guys?!"

"Don't make it worse," Judy warned him. "I had my suspicions before I heard from Neal. You couldn't expect someone like Lewis not to rat you out, could you?" She added a few choice insults, then turned her back on Remmy and said blandly to Neal, "We didn't want the Costa Rican authorities to get here before we could. Jurisdiction often comes down to who gets there first, and I'm not letting that asshole slip through my fingers again."

Scarlet had appeared at Neal's side without his notice, a fact that would have alarmed him with anyone else. "Well, we certainly appreciate having this mess cleaned up as quickly as possible," she said, all business. "This way, please."

Not one of the soldiers had a problem accepting her authority and falling into step behind her, each of them giving Neal a grin and a not-so-gentle punch in the shoulder as they went past. All except Remmy, who only glared.

"I can't believe you'd take his word over mine," Remmy grumbled. "You don't even know where he's been for ten years."

Judy was the last to pass, and she alone stopped at Neal, and after a moment of staring at him, broke into a grin and enfolded him into a fierce hug. "You son of a bitch," she said fondly. "You could have called sooner, you know. They've got phones here, I hear."

She stepped back and inspected Mary with critical eyes.

Neal wanted instinctively to step between them, but paused.

Mary swallowed. "How do you do," she said formally. "I'm…"

"You're Neal's mate," Judy finished for her. "That's good enough for me."

Without further formality, she gave Mary a punch in the shoulder and turned to follow the rest of the team into the courtyard where Scarlet had Lewis and his men lined up in duct tape restraints.

Mary rubbed her shoulder and turned mystified eyes to Neal.

"Sorry," Neal said. "Judy takes a little getting used to."

"I like her," Mary said, with a surprisingly large smile.

$\mathcal{T}$he courtyard was crowded with nearly a dozen restrained men, Neal's team, and Scarlet's staff. Tex, Travis, and Bastian seemed to feel that the handover required their direct supervision, and Benedict, who was not restrained, kept wringing his hands and muttering about his lawyer.

Judy gave Lewis a toothy smile, clearly enjoying his furious sulk.

"I told you I'd be back for you, you bastard."

"I should be so flattered," Lewis snarled back. "You're only here because Neal went whining for his *girlfriend* to come and save him."

"And he did a fine job before we even got here," Judy answered, not in the slightest ruffled. "Because you're an incompetent jackass who surrounds himself with other incompetent jackasses and turncoats and then wonders why you can't inspire loyalty."

"How did you get free of your guards?" Tex asked in an undertone as Judy talked about the legal details of taking custody of Scarlet's prisoners.

"Gizelle," Neal said. "Er, the gazelle. I've been calling her Gizelle in my head. I have no idea what her name really is."

"What, did she skewer one of them?"

"Turned into a human and hypnotized them," Neal said with a sideways smile.

"Neat trick!" Tex said.

"Not as neat as a 'forget-me field'," Travis scoffed. "Seriously, Bastian, what was that? You didn't think that was just a little bit impossible?"

"We've already had this discussion," Bastian said with mock seriousness. "You just don't remember it."

"We want to get these guys back on American soil as soon as possible," Judy said, concluding her discussion with Scarlet. "So we'd best get going."

"You're welcome back any time," Scarlet said warmly.

"I thought the resort was for shifters only," Judy said with a searching look. "We're not all shifters."

"We can make exceptions," Scarlet said with a meaningful look in return. "Any of your team is welcome to stay here."

"Does that team include you, Neal?" Judy's voice was a challenge, and Mary felt Neal's hand tighten in hers.

But Neal shook his head. "Not any more," he said, and Mary could hear the mixture of regret and determination in his voice. "I've got a lot of healing left to do, and I'm ready to settle down and do what needs to be done. No more hiding."

Mary felt a little surge of relief. She would never have asked him to give up his team, but she knew that she'd have a hard time being away from him during his missions, missing and worrying for him.

"We'll miss you," Judy said frankly, clasping his arm.

"We *have* missed you. But I'm not surprised. I'll be back for that drink and the story you owe me."

Neal let go of Mary's hand to embrace her. "I'll be waiting," he said hoarsely.

Judy turned to Mary. "Take good care of him," she said firmly.

Mary drew herself up. "I intend to," she said just as firmly.

CHAPTER 38

$\mathcal{N}$eal woke with a start, disoriented, until he realized that he wasn't in his own bed. He was snuggled up close to Mary's warm, curvy form.

Part of the disorientation was that he hadn't woken from nightmares, but from sweet, restful sleep, for the first night that he could remember.

Sunlight spilled around the edges of the curtains covering the big glass doors at the foot of Mary's bed, and she stirred as Neal sat up.

"I am never taking clean sheets for granted again," Mary purred, as she stretched and opened her eyes.

Neal couldn't find words to answer her, just taking in the beautiful curves of her body under the silky sheet, and the splay of her hair on the pillow. She smiled up at him, and Neal could read the warmth and affection in her expression.

She felt like home. Like safety and wholeness and happiness. Like forever and happy endings and things that Neal had never guessed he could claim for himself.

He was still staring at her, he realized, as her expression became quizzical.

"I'm glad you could get your plane tickets changed," he said. It was the truth, if not the whole truth.

"I feel so terrible for the substitute. A whole week of those students, all wound up from spring break." Mary chuckled. "But not terrible enough to regret it."

"I should have my visa sorted in time to go back with you," Neal said, and he was glad of it. He wasn't sure he could stand watching Mary get on a plane without him.

"What do you want to do this week?" Mary asked.

"I… guess I figured I'd keep working," Neal said, blinking. He hadn't really considered himself a guest at the resort, though he supposed that Scarlet's invitation to stay on as a guest had included him. "And you'd enjoy the pool."

"I was thinking we might go parasailing," Mary suggested shyly. "And maybe snorkeling? It seems like a shame to come all the way to Costa Rica just to sit by a pool."

Neal grinned at her. "We could go hiking."

Mary hit him with a pillow, and Neal caught it easily, reaching to wrestle her down and tickle her.

"I have a better idea," they said in one breath to each other.

His mouth on hers was the perfect ending.

A NOTE FROM ZOE CHANT

I hope you enjoyed Neal and Mary's book! Thank you so much for reading it!

I always love to know what you thought – you can leave a review at Amazon (I read every one, and they help other readers find me, too!) or email me at zoechantebooks@gmail.com.

If you'd like to be emailed when I release my next book, please click here to be added to my mailing list. You can also visit my webpage, or follow me on Facebook. You are also invited to join my VIP Readers Group on Facebook, where I show off new covers first, and you can get sneak previews and ask questions.

Keep reading for a preview chapter from the next book in the Shifting Sands Resort series, *Tropical Bartender Bear*, where Tex finds his mate!

The cover of *Tropical Wounded Wolf* was designed by Ellen Million (visit her page to find coloring pages of some of my characters, including Gizelle and Graham!).

MORE FROM ZOE CHANT

Shifting Sands Resort: A complete ten-book series - plus two collections of shorts. This is a sizzling shifter romance set at a tropical island resort. Each book stands alone but connects into a great mystery with a thrilling conclusion. Start with Tropical Tiger Spy or dive in to the Omnibus edition, with all of the novels, short stories, and novellas in my preferred reading order! Shifting Sands Resort crosses over with Shifter Kingdom and Fire and Rescue Shifters.

∼

Fae Shifter Knights: A complete four-book fantasy portal romp, with cute pets and swoon-worthy knights stuck in a world of wonders like refrigerators and ham sandwiches. Start with Dragon of Glass!

∼

Green Valley Shifters: A sweet, small town series with single dads, secret shifters, sweet kids, and spinsters. Low-peril and steamy! Standalone books where you can revisit your favorite characters - this series is also complete with six books! Start with Dancing Bearfoot! This series crosses over with **Virtue Shifters**, which starts with Timber Wolf.

WRITING AS ELVA BIRCH

The Royal Dragons of Alaska: A fascinating alternate world where Alaska is ruled by secret dragon shifters. Adventure, romance, and humor! Reluctant royalty, relentless enemies…dogs, camping, and magic! Start with The Dragon Prince of Alaska.

∼

Suddenly Shifters: A hilarious series of novellas, serials, and shorts set in the small town of Anders Canyon, where something (in the water?) is making ordinary citizens turn into shifters. Start with Something in the Water! Also available in audio!

∼

Birch Hearts: An enchanting collection of short stories and novellas. Unconstrained by theme or setting, each short read has romance, magic, and heart, with a satisfying conclusion. And always, the impossible and irresistible.

Start with a sampler plate in Prompted 2 for fourteen pieces of sweet-to-sizzling flash fiction, or the novella, Better Half. Breakup is a free story!

A Day Care for Shifters: A hot new full-length series about adorable shifter kids and their struggling single parents in a town full of mystery and surprise. Start the series with Wolf's Instinct, when Addison comes to Nickel City to take a job at a very special day care and finds a family to belong to. Funny and full of feeling, this is a gentle ice-cream-straight-from-the-container escape. Sweet and sizzling!

SUPPORT ME ON PATREON

What is Patreon?

Patreon is a site where readers and fans can support creators with monthly subscriptions.

At my Patreon, I have tiers with early rough drafts of my books, flash fiction, coloring pages, signed and sketched paperbacks, exclusive swag, original artwork, photographs…and so much more! Every month is a little different, and there is a price for every budget. Patreon allows me to do projects that aren't very commercial and makes my income stream a little less unpredictable. It also gives me a place to connect with my fans!

Come find out what's going on behind the scenes and keep me creating at Patreon! patreon.com/ellenmillion

THE BOOK I WASN'T WRITING

To win his mate, he'll have to put his foot down.

Anita is tickled pink when billionaire Frank Wilson picks her little bakery to provide desserts for The Wet and Wild Charity Gala. But what was supposed to be the opportunity of a lifetime turns into the storm of a century.

Flamingo shifter and philanthropist, Frank has been going through life like one of his own clockwork sculptures, not sure of his purpose until he meets the plucky baker who captures his heart and assumes he's a janitor. Trapped together with his fated mate in a big, empty (possibly haunted) event hall with two thousand gourmet cupcakes and no power, Frank is sure that nothing could stand between him and his ultimate happiness.

The only problem is, she's not interested in completing his flock…

…and they aren't alone in the building.

I love to do harmless April Fool's Day pranks, and I made this cover for my readers, even going so far as to make a book blurb and fake Amazon book preview image for Facebook.

But the joke was on me and this, of all of the books I had planned, was the one I had the most readers clamoring for!

I swore I wasn't writing it, but shared sneak previews and excerpts with my readers and I finished released it as a surprise on April 1 the following year. You can read it here!

If you would like to read snippets of the sequel I'm very *definitely* not writing, you'll have to sign up for my mailing list or join my Reader's Retreat at Facebook!

SNEAK PREVIEW OF THE DRAGON PRINCE OF ALASKA...

Writing as Elva Birch.

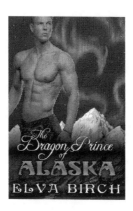

Carina Andresen surged to her feet, sweeping her camp chair out from under her as a make-shift weapon.

Wolf! her brain hammered at her. *Wolf!* She was going to become an Alaska tourist statistic and get eaten by a wolf on her second week in the kingdom.

Logic slowly caught up with her panic.

The animal across the campfire from her was smaller and *doggier* than a wolf, and it was only a moment before Carina could get her breath and heartbeat back under control and recognize that it was well-groomed, shyly eyeing her sizzling hot dog, and wagging its tail.

Alaska probably had stray dogs, too; she wasn't *that* far from civilization.

"Hi there, sweetie," Carina said, her voice still unnaturally high as she put her chair back on its legs. "Does that smell good? Want a bit of hot dog?" Carina turned the hot dog in the flame and waggled it suggestively.

The non-edible dog sped up his tail and when Carina broke off a piece of the meat and dropped it beside her, he crept around the fire and slurped it eagerly up off the ground.

The second bite he took gently from her fingers, and by the second hot dog she dared to pet him.

Within about thirty minutes and five hot dogs, he was leaning on her and letting her scratch his ears and neck as he wagged his tail and groaned in delight.

"Oh, you're just a dear," Carina said. "I bet someone's missing you." He was a husky mix, Carina guessed; he was tall and strong, with a long, thick coat of dark gray fur and white feet. His ears were upright, and his tail was long and feathered. He didn't have a collar, but he was clearly friendly. "You want some water?"

The dog licked his lips as if he had understood, and Carina carefully stood so she didn't frighten him.

But he seemed to be past any shyness now, and he followed Carina to her van trustingly, tail waving happily. He drank the offered water from a frying pan, and then tried to give Carina a kiss dripping with slobber.

"You probably already have a name," Carina said, laughingly trying to escape the wet tongue. "But I'm going to call you Shadow for now." She had a grubby towel hanging from her clothesline and used it to dry off his face. They played a gentle game of tug-of-war, testing each other's strength and manners.

Shadow seemed to approve of his new name and gave her a canine grin once she'd won the towel back from him.

"Alright, Shadow, let's go collect some more firewood."

The area was rich with downed wood to harvest, and with the assistance of a folding hand saw, Carina was able to find several heaping armloads of solid, dry wood, enough to keep a cheerful fire going for a few days if she was frugal. It was comforting to have Shadow around for the task; she wasn't quite as nervous about the noises she heard, and he was a happy distraction from her own brain.

He frolicked with her, and found a stick three times his own length to drag around possessively.

"So helpful!" Carina laughed at him, as he knocked over an empty pot and swiped her across the knees so that she nearly fell.

When she sat down beside the crackling fire in her low camp chair, Shadow abandoned his prize stick and crowded close to lay his head on her knee. Carina petted him absently.

"Someone's looking for you, you big softy," she said regretfully. She would have to try to reunite the dog with his owner but, for now, it was nice having a companion around the camp.

Of all the things she expected when she went running for the wilderness, she had never guessed that the silence would be the worst. She had been camping plenty, but it was always *with* someone. Since their parents had died, that someone was usually her sister, June, but sometimes it was a friend or a roommate. She was used to having someone to point out birds and animals to, someone to share chores with, stretch out tarps with. When it was just her, the spaces seemed vaster, the wind bit harder, and even the birds were less cheerful.

"You probably don't care about the birds that would make my life list," she told Shadow mournfully.

Shadow wagged his tail in a rustle of leaves.

She didn't have her life list anymore to add to anyway.

Everything had been left behind: her phone, her computer, her identity. Her entire life was on hold. She had the van to live in, some supplies and a small nest egg to start from, so she ought to be able to stay out of sight long enough to regroup and...she didn't know what to do from here. Find a journalist willing to take her story and clear her name?

To fill the quiet, and to help ignore the ache in her chest, she read aloud from the brochure on Alaska that she had been given at the border station. She'd found it that evening while she was emptying the glovebox to take stock of supplies, and Shadow seemed as good a listener as any.

"Like many modern monarchies, Alaska has an elected council of officials who do most of the day to day rulings of this vast, rich land. The royal family is steeped in tradition and mystery, and holds many veto powers, as well as acting as ambassadors to other countries. Known as the Dragon King, the Alaskan sovereign is a reserved figure who rarely appears in public. Margaret, the Queen of Alaska, died twelve years ago, leaving behind six sons." There was a photo, with boys ranging from about seven to maybe twenty-five. Two of the middle children were identical. One of the twins was wearing a hockey jersey and grinning, the other wore glasses and looked annoyed. The oldest—or at least the tallest—was frowning seriously at the others. The only blonde of the bunch was one of the middle boys, who was looking intently at the camera. The youngest looked painfully bored. They all had tongue-twisting names of more syllables than Carina wanted to try pronouncing.

Carina thought it was an interesting photo. The tension between the oldest two was palpable, and the they were all dressed surprisingly casually. She didn't follow royal gossip much beyond scanning headlines at grocery store checkouts, but Alaska never seemed to make waves; they were rarely involved in dramas and scandals.

Shadow raised his head and cocked his head at some imagined noise in the forest.

"That's a lot of siblings," Carina observed, ruffling his ears. She felt so much safer having him beside her. "Just one sister was more than enough for me." She didn't want to admit how much she missed that sister right now.

Shadow returned his head to her knee. "Alaska is a member of the Small Kingdoms Alliance, an exclusive collective of independent monarchies scattered throughout the world. Although Alaska has large amounts of land, they qualify for membership because of their small population."

Carina turned the brochure over. "There are hot springs about fifty miles north of Fairbanks! I hope to make it there." *Before* she ran out of cash. It looked expensive. Maybe she could get work there...she'd heard that it wasn't hard to find under-the-table jobs in this country.

Shadow suddenly leapt to his feet, barking at something crashing through the woods behind them and Carina nearly tipped over backwards in her camp chair trying to stand up.

She expected to find a moose, or possibly a bear, and she was already picking up the chair to use as a flimsy defense against a charging wild animal.

But it was only a man stepping out of the woods, in an official dark blue uniform emblazoned with the eight gold stars of Alaska.

For a moment, terror every bit as keen as the panic that had gripped her at the first sight of Shadow washed over her. They'd found her.

"You're trespassing on royal land and I'm going to have to ask you to leave," he said.

Then she realized with relief that it wasn't a police officer. He was only a park ranger.

...or was he? Discover love and adventure in a wonderful alternate Alaska with camping and dogs and magic, reluctant royalty and relentless enemies! Pick up The Dragon Prince of Alaska *today!*

Made in the USA
Coppell, TX
29 March 2024

30689880R00107